BLACK, WHITE & BROWN ON THE BLUE LINE

BY

ODIE HAWKINS

AuthorHouse™ LLC
1663 Liberty Drive
Bloomington, IN 47403
www.authorhouse.com
Phone: 1-800-839-8640

Front and back photos by Zola Salena-Hawkins
www.flickr.com/photos/32886903@N02

Cover designs by AuthorHouse Design Team.

Published by AuthorHouse 12/12/13

ISBN: 978-1-4918-4484-7 (sc)
ISBN: 978-1-4918-4483-0 (e)

Library of Congress Control Number: 2013922762

BLACK, WHITE AND BROWN ON THE BLUE LINE

*DEDICATED TO ROYLENE LOVELY WALKER,
WHOSE BRAINS AND VISION MADE THIS BOOK A REALITY.
TO MERILENE M. MURPHY,
A BRIGHT SUN WARMING THIS COLD WORLD.
TO P. K. "CASH", COMMODITIES BROKER,
FOR SHOWING ME WHERE THE MONEY IS.*

*TO THE WATTS PROPHETS, AMDE TZION HAMILTON,
RICHARD DEDEAUX AND OTIS O'SOLOMON
FOR THEIR TALENT, STRENGTH AND DETERMINATION.*

*TO THE CONCERNED ARTISTS ACTION GROUP
FOR THEIR COURAGE TO DO THE RIGHT THING.*

*AND TO THE BROTHERS AND SISTERS
RIDING THE BLUE LINE.*

ADUPE . . .

Prologue . . .

It would have been impossible to predict a Blue Line in Los Angeles, Watts, 107th and Avalon Avenue, California when I came to live there, back in 1966.

In Los Angeles County, many of us, pressed by circumstances, have suffered distances that would make a camel thirsty. Or cause a new car to need an oil change.

There were people talking about putting trains on city tracks, no doubt. But I never heard their talk; I was too busy trying to force my raggedy ol' car to run a few more miles. Or trying to figure out how I could walk from Belgium to Holland without peeing on myself.

(Once upon a time, stranded beside a road to Eternity, down there in Orange County, someone told me that the property I was standing in front of was as large as Luxembourg. And I had walked across most of Austria to get there).

Gotta admit it, I didn't have the vision to assume that there would ever be a railed transportation system, like our hard heeled CTA in Chicago. Certainly, nothing that would ever come close to that monstrosity that connects various tentacles of New York with itself.

The Blue Line 21st Century,(and it's crossing arms, the Green and Red Lines) is unique. It doesn't go very far; surely there's more railway at Disneyland, but it does take you to different places, if your mind is open.

From the Metro station, 7th Street, Downtown Los Angeles, to 1st Street, Downtown Long Beach. From the end of one world to the end of another world.

Rich people do not ride the Blue Line, meaning that the Blue Line is there for people of color who are not wealthy. A hard-core of White, working types ride the train in the morning, going to their jobs in downtown Los Angeles and again in the evenings.

There is a heavy police presence (the train has it's own special police force), heavy. Lots of money invested in the Blue Line and none of the investors want to lose anything because of people being afraid to ride the train, or gang warfare.

Strangely, the honor system is in effect. Signs in English, Spanish and Korean explain that each passenger should have proof of payment; if not, the penalty is a stiff fine.

No eating, drinking, smoking or outrageous behavior is permitted, and the rules are seriously enforced.

Sometimes, for days on end, riding north and south, south and north, no one will check to see who has a ticket, a transfer or a bus pass (for train travel too), but the seed of obedience to the rules has been so deeply sowed that most sensible people know that it isn't worth the gamble to try to cheat the system.

African-Americans and Spanish speaking Brown-skinned people ride the Blue Line. ***BLACK AND BROWN ON THE BLUE LINE ETC.*** comes from our experiences with each other.

CHAPTER ONE

Babies/Infantile Thoughts (From 7th to Pico) . . .

Babies, so many babies. Black and Brown babies, babies with attitudes, stoic babies, squawking babies, smiling babies, drooling babies, silly babies, laughing babies, funny babies, sad babies, frightened babies, fearless babies, sick babies, healthy babies, sleeping babies, clean babies, dirty babies, spoiled babies, unspoiled babies, little babies, big babies, all beautiful.

The babies are usually carried, but often pushed into the train in a stroller by women. But, from time to time, a man enters the vehicle with a baby in his arms.

It would be emotionally dishonest to suggest that I was never attracted to babies, I think all curious people are attracted to these unusual creatures.

The Blue Line offered me my first moving study of babies; their relationship to the person (persons) they are with, their relationship to themselves and the world at large.

Sadly, I must confess that I had to be cautious about how I looked at these innocent people. In today's evil world there are people who would do harm to babies, and I never want to be mistaken for one of them.

For that reason alone I was never able to make friends with any of the Blue Line babies. I feared the consequences of being too warm, too loving, too charmed by the babies.

Yes, that's what the world has come to. The men and women, however, who hold the babies in their arms seem to have an ambiguous attitude about friendly attention. They seem to like someone's admiring glance or a friendly, "0, how cute she/he is," but we were all too conscious of the mean spirits swirling around to feel totally at ease.

I sat in place, stared whenever I dared and made mental notes.

The almond eyes of an eight month old clinched eyes with me. She has an absolutely round face and head and the look of a clairvoyant. She does not blink and seems to know something.

Eight months old. What can she possibly know? I'm fascinated by the intelligence of her expression. She looks more intelligent than her mother and father even.

I'm tempted to speak to her, to ask her serious questions about the world she just came from, but there is no need to disturb our telepathic communication, just to say some words.

Her mother, a small, beautifully sculpted lady, who has the profile of a face from an ancient Mayan wall, notices our exchange and smiles.

Her smile seems to say, "Ahhhh yes, she is a deep child."

I have to break the lock she has on my attention by staring out of the window for a few beats. I've had a couple of cats pull me into their psychic modes for spans of the time, the same way that the baby is doing. It's the opaqueness of their eyes, that seems to whisper everything you've ever wanted to hear.

I turn back to discover that the mother, the father and the baby have disappeared. I make a quick, surreptitious search around the train. They're not there. We haven't come to the next station, they couldn't've gotten off the train.

I'm forced to settle back and relax. Don't panic, simply the subject matter buzzing through my head that's responsible for me imagining that I saw this baby. Just of my imagination. Yeah, right . . .

*   *   *

"The sleepers," I dubbed them, these extraordinary beings who have developed the ability to sleep through this world's chaos. How did they learn how to do it, at such an early age? Years later, rich people spend thousands of dollars, yeh, pesos, naira, cedis, pesetas, shekels, to find gurus to teach them how to do what babies do.

I stared at the baby, carefully noting the classic I-am-happy-smile. Ten paces beyond its stroller, within easy grasp of its mother's protective-shielding arms, within the danger zone of a piece of social dynamite, the baby slept.

Ten of us, at least, were mentally/psychologically preparing ourselves to take the social dynamite down, if not out, if he got a micron too close to the smiling sleeper.

Fortunately, for him, he popped off at the next stop, cussin' 'n screaming!

The ten of us (it might have been twenty, counting the men) breathed a sigh of pure relief. Now, we won't have to lynch a person-with-problems who was threatening Baby-Space. Babydom was secure.

Suzuki (the Zen guy, not the motor guy), Ferlinghetti, and the hip Alan Ginsberg, knew a lot about Zen and being cool, but what did they know about sleeping babies on the Blue Line?

Day after day, I looked up from my reading of "Them is Me" and "whatever that may be, is" and stared into the sleeping awake eyes of hundreds of "sleepers."

Don't they know what's happening in Congo, Bosnia, Ireland, New Zealand, Russia, China, Hong Kong, Texas, Australia, Antarctica, Spain, New Jersey? Don't they realize the consequences of their sleeping?

Maybe they do, maybe they don't. We (been here much longer now) could easily rationalize what we understand about cool behavior by understanding how **not** cool behavior equates to nasty behavior. Usually.

"The Sleepers" have obviously worked themselves past all of this stuff.

They go to sleep when they're sleepy, and it's quite obvious to anyone who studies geopolitics, science, industry, economics, race relations, or any of the other Earthbound disciplines, that sleep is the ultimate solution to most of our shit.

Sad babies, funny babies, addicted babies. My daughter, Gabrielle, a mother, is responsible for revealing the natural addiction that babies are prone to suffer.

"What do you think that 2:00 A.M. feeding thing is all about?"

It makes all the sense in the world to me, this junkie pattern of behavior. They are not always hungry when they demand to be fed every four-five hours, maybe it's something in the baby food.

Once again, Gabrielle points out, "Ever notice the difference between breast-fed babies and bottle-fed babies?"

I had to confess that I hadn't paid that much attention.

"Well, check it out. Generally speaking, the breastfed doesn't seem to need as many feedings. They sleep sounder, give their parents more rest.

"The bottle fed baby has to have it NOW! And if they don't get it? . . . Well, you've seen the tantrums and all of that other negative behavior."

What's in that formula anyway? Won't it be heart rending, twenty years from now, when some independent scientist reveals the secret ingredients that hooked our babies and created a junkie mentality for the rest of our lives?

The stoic ones most often hold my attention longest. What's on their minds? What are they thinking about as they stare at this world they've just recently tumbled into head first?

Such a sophisticated expression for a year old face. How could they have learned how to be so cool in such a short time?

The babies with attitudes (see the Mussolini jut of the jaw and the pushed out bottom lip?), the squawking babies, the drooler, the silly ones, the delighted-with-life-laughing ones (what is in that formula?), the frightened babies, the fearless babies who will stick their hands into a Rotweiler's mouth, or whip a rattlesnake around by the tail, the sick babies, the healthy babies, the clean and dirty ones, the spoiled, unspoiled ones and the big ones, all beautiful, all delightful mysteries. What are they going to become?

*   *   *

Artesia Station . . .

They were obviously upper-middle class Anglos who were being forced to ride the train, probably for the first time. It was obvious in every move they made, every glazed, blue eyed look they gave the Black and Brown people on the train.

A tall, blonde, blue eyed man, the father, a shorter, blue eyed brunette, the mother, and a boy and girl who were almost Xerox copies of their parents.

They formed a private kraal with the two seats they occupied. The parents held the children in their laps as though they were going to escape or be captured.

The two children, full of Sugar Pops and White bread-Anglo upraising, squirmed uncontrollably, unaccustomed to being restricted by their parents. And while they squirmed, they released a stream of revealing commentary.

"Ooohh Mom! Look It's a river!"

"That's not really a river, Judy, that's kind of a large drainage ditch . . . water . . ."

"You were right, Dad, there's a lot of niggers 'n spics on the train."

The father pretended that he hadn't heard his son say what he had said, and at the same time slipped a garden—calloused hand over the boy's mouth.

"The niggers 'n spics on the train," their racial remotes already tuned to the scene, exchanged sarcastic expression.

"Which ones are the niggers 'n which ones are the spics?" Judy asked her manually silenced brother.

Her brother squirmed and tried to pull his father's hand from his mouth. He succeeded.

"Stop! Stop it, Dad, I can't breathe!"

The parents had developed a fiery glow on both sides of their faces and at the back of their necks. They gave the impression of having been stricken by hot flashes.

"Uhhh, what time is it, Sally?" the father asked his wife, ignoring his own watch.

"Um, approximately, 4:12 .. .uhh . . . 4:13."

The children exchanged puzzled expressions. They were not sure of what to make of their parent's behavior.

"Look, Judy, Bud! Look down there! You can see cars on the freeway."

Their voices had a nervous, metallic edge, a bit too loud. The other people on the train, those who were within hearing range, paid close attention.

A young White woman who had been pretending to read a book was now pretending to take a nap.

"Mommy, which ones are the gangbangers?"

The sheer velocity of the children's questions ruled out the possibility of stifling them.

The reddish glow on the parent's cheeks spread to their suddenly moist foreheads. "How long is it going to take for us to get to the Metro transfer point, f' Godsakes!?"

"Yeh, Dad, where are the gangbangers?"

And now we're at the Imperial station where all of the baggiest pants, the most bizarre hair styles and the creme de la creme of gansta rap, Hip Hop fashion piles on, complete with a style of talking that was once considered low, even in the low places.

The two teenaged brothers, one cue balled, the other braided, carried on a conversation that they had started on the station platform.

"So, hey, I tol' the bitch she could suck my motherfuckin' dick, you know what I mean?!"

"You shoulda kicked that bitch's ass!"

A middle aged African-American woman, with a look of intense sadness, leaned her grey head against the window. My sons . . .

The White couple and their children stared at the mouths of the two young men talking, shocked speechless.

"I did kick her fuckin' ass! but that was last week, this was about suckin' my dick, you know what I mean?"

An older African-American man, with hard lines in his face, and tobacco stains on his teeth, leaned across the aisle and spoke to the White couple in a firm baritone.

"These are not niggers, spics or gangbangers. These are our children."

The gray haired sister turned in the direction of his voice and nodded in agreement.

"Fuck you think she did?"

*   *   *

We Ain't All Mexican, Brothers . . .

The chocolate brown face was as flexible as a dramatist's pen, but it only reflected distress. The distress was caused by the sounds that rippled all around him.

He glanced at the profile of the beige skinned woman sitting beside him, who was talking to her girlfriend across the aisle, and frowned.

And the frown deepened as the conversations mostly in Spanish, bobbed and weaved around his ears. Clearly, this fifty year old African-American man with the salt and pepper mustache and hair was annoyed.

He glanced with relief as the woman sitting beside him stood to exit the train. His glance of relief gave way to a smile of welcome as an African-American man, perhaps ten years his junior, slid into the seat that the woman had vacated.

They nodded to each other as the brothers will do, when they are acknowledging each other's presence.

The rippling conversations in Spanish seemed to escalate at the Compton station. The older man began to do a solovoice grumble, tacitly assuming that the man sitting next to him was an ally, or at least neutral. The older man released his grousy commentary from the corner of his mouth, San Quentin prison—style.

"That's all I hear, day in 'n day out, Spanoli, Spanoli, Spanoli, Spanoli . . . It's like this ain't even America no mo'. You don't even hear English, 'less you goin' to school or somethin'."

He paused to take a hard look at the profile of the man seated next to him, as though to measure the level of interest the man was showing. The man's mental expression was an incentive for him to continue his low level complaining.

"They takin' our jobs, O.K.? You hear what I'm saying, they takin' our jobs."

The younger man, a darker version of the man who was complaining, turned to look at his seatmate. It was the spur that the older man needed.

"That's right, they takin' our jobs. Pretty soon, the whole place will be Mexican. What about that?"

The "question" was more an affirmation of the man's question, than the quest for an answer.

"Well, my friend, I don' know about that."

"And them that ain't takin' our jobs is on welfare, bleedin' us, the American taxpayer to death . . . ."

"I don' theenk . . ."

"Too many babies, hell, just look around you, looks like most of these Mexican women is having three babies a year . . . ."

The older man overpowered the younger man's attempt to speak.

"Too many babies! You hear what I'm sayin'? Too many babies. Pretty soon the whole state ain't gon' be nothin' but Mexicans."

"Look, my friend, I don' agree with what you are sayin'."

The complainer stared at his seatmate.

"Sounds like you got a lil' bit o' an accent yourself. Where you from?"

"Ha-bana."

"Ha-bana? Where's that?"

"Coo-ba," the man answered with a big smile.

The complainer turned to stare out at the cityscape flickering by and muttered, "Damn! You one of 'em too."

"We ain't all Mexican, brother", the man replied in his slightly accented English.

CHAPTER TWO

The Gangbanger and the Fool, a Detour . . .

He stomped onto the train eating, (curling his right forefinger into a can of crabmeat); that's a no no, punishable by a $250 fine. He was cussing some imaginary figure in his life. He may have been high from something or other, but maybe not; he was all of the negative stuff, that's what the vibes radiating from his hard shell told us.

We tightened our emotional seat belts; we were going to be forced to go a few stations with a Nasty One.

The Nasty One seems to be an "EL-A" phenomenon, it may have something to do with the distances and the vibes that the neighborhoods cast off on the vehicles rolling through. It can get downright messy on the Western Avenue bus going south or the Wilshire bus going east or west.

The Nasty One (infrequently two) is not as often experienced on the Blue Line, the Metro cops sift out most of the rough riders, but occasionally a Nasty will slip through.

Medium tall, brown skinned man, about thirtyish needing a shave and a bath. There was nothing about him that was intimidating, other than the grating sound of his voice.

Collectively, the few Whites reddened, stared harder at their newspapers/books, and gave every sign of praying that the police would pop onto the train at the next station. The Brown people ignored him, just another Negro loco. The Black people were trying to wish him away. The wish was like a stiff breeze blowing through the train.

No one wanted to tell him to shut up and sit down. No one cared enough about him to say anything to him, and it fed him jolts of insecurity.

"So, what did I say?! I said 'fuck 'im.' That what I said 'fuck 'im.'"

A clever, attention seeking fool. He turned his rhetoric down to a whisper as the train paused to admit new passengers and discharged old ones, doing a quick scan to determine if there were undercover cops on the scene.

Satisfied that he wasn't being spied on, he revved himself back up as soon as the doors closed and the train eased on down the track.

"Yeah! Fuck 'im and fuck yo' momma too. Yeahhh, that's what I said!"

"Hey man, why don't you stop usin' all that bad language 'n shit around these women 'n children 'n shit 'n sit yo' ass down somewhere?"

The voice was coming from the seat in front of me. It was a silky voice, but strong and definite.

The Nasty One paused in his parade through the aisle, blinking in surprise. We were all surprised. The surprise stemmed from the source of the voice.

A young brother, his pants as low on his butt as they could possibly be without dropping to his knees, was the speaker.

"What?! What?! You talkin' to me young niggah?!"

The young man, muffled in his Mount Everest gansta rap jacket, twisted his eyes to make a peripheral glare. Seated behind him, I took note of the malevolence of his walleyed threat.

He didn't move his head as he answered, "Yeah, I'm talkin' to you. I said . . . why don't you sit yo' ass down somewhere?"

Two young Black women, red nailed and stylishly coiffed, their waistlines and belly buttons fashionably bared, stared at the young man with the silky voice.

The Nasty One immediately sat on the first seat he could find, the elderly-handicapped seat beside the door, blustering in a softer tone!

"Who the fuck you think you are?! How you gon' tell me what to do?"

The young man rose half-way from his seat and made a waistband adjustment. It was impossible, from my angle to see what he was adjusting.

"I just said you oughta stop usin' all that foul language 'n shit! That's want I said. You wanna make something outta that?!"

Incredibly, a clean field between the two people opened like something had cleaved it. It was "Git down time" and the Nasty One instantly reverted to being the Fool, the Clown who didn't really mean anybody harm.

"Awwww, hold on now, young brother . . . looks like you wanna take this seriously. I mean, c'mon now, ain't no sense in takin' this too seriously. You know what I mean?

"Now I know you a gangbanger 'n all that but you don't have to take it out on me . . . ."

The Fool (formerly a Nasty One) pushed his voice into the begging zone by elevating his tones to a higher level. The fear that drove him to cop a plea was almost comical, it showed in his rapidly blinking eyes.

"All I'm saying to you is this, shut the fuck up!"

"Hey, you got it, my brother . . . whatever you say."

The train slid into the Florence station without another word being spoken by anyone.

*   *   *

Familiar Strangers

It's a sociological term, "familiar strangers," and maybe a concept too.

Lots of familiar strangers ride the Blue Line every day. We see each other but we don't know each other.

The El Salvadorians see the Mexicans, the Mexicans see the Koreans, the African-Americans see the Hondurans, the Whites see the Panamanians, but no one really knows anything about anybody else, unless they've taken the time to make the extraordinary effort to find out who the familiar strangers are.

It was a gentlemanly thing to do when the books and papers slipped out of her hands and splashed at his-feet, he bent down to gather up the spill.

"Oh, thank you."

"No problem."

He made a neat package of the papers and handed it to her. The other passengers took note of his chivalry and smiled with approval.

The young woman held the notebooks and papers in her lap, leaned her head against the window of the train and nodded off again. The young man seated next to her surreptitiously studied her profile.

This is a fine sister here.

Her full lips and long eyelashes held his attention longest, and the voluptuous, but shapely figure inside the nurse's white coat and pants.

The books and papers slid from her lap again. Again, the gentleman bent to pick them up.

"0 thank you, I'm sorry . . . ."

"Ain't no problem, no problem at all . . . ."

He made an orderly job of it, pausing to make certain that he was placing things in the order she had dropped them in.

"That's O.K.," he answered and directed his attention to the passing scenes. Yeahh, this is a really fine sister here. What is she, a Mexican?

Two stations later she stood to exit, offering her tight white smile.

"'Scuse me, this is my place."

"This is where you get off, huh?"

"Yes."

"Awright, take it easy now and hold on tight to your books 'n stuff."

The sound of her clean belled laughter fluttered back to him as she made her exit.

He waved to her as she walked past his window, she waved back, and made a little drama of clutching her books to her breasts.

*   *   *

Herb slumped down into the worn interior of his mother's easy chair, indulgently remoting from one channel to another.

"Stupid ass people putting all of their business in the streets. Wonder how much they get paid for spilling their guts like this?"

"He knew I was a transsexual."

"How did he know?"

"'Cause T told him!"

"Well, how did it go today?"

Herb popped out of his slump.

"Oh, hi, moms, you caught me checkin' the freakies out again."

"Yeah, you have to be careful of that stuff, it can become addicting. Put Oprah on. Well, how did it go?"

Herb remoted Oprah Winfrey on and clicked the volume way down.

"Not good, not bad. I went to a few places, filled out applications 'n stuff. This one place looks promising, I had a chance to talk with the manager and he didn't seem to be too upset about me havin' a record.

"You're a young man," he said, "a young man will make mistakes. I was a young man once myself."

"That's what he said. It don't mean that he's gonna hire me but he sounded sympathetic anyway."

"Well, that's better than nothin'. You eat yet?"

"Nawww, I was waitin' for you to come."

She patted him on the cheek and strolled to the kitchen.

"Turn Oprah up a bit while I'm in here. I'll fix us a couple of sandwiches."

Herb remoted the sound of Oprah Winfrey's show up and settled back, his mind miles away from the scene in front of him.

That sure was a fine young lady on the train today, a fine young lady.

He gazed around the room. Mom's really likes to keep things neat.

"Herb, you want lemonade or milk?"

"Lemonade or milk? She must still think I'm ten years old. Forty ounces would be more my style.

"Uhhh, lemonade is O.K., Moms."

He took a hard look at his mother as she re-entered the room with a tray of sandwiches and two tall glasses of lemonade. She placed the tray on a cocktail table and sat on the sofa near her son.

Mom must've been a beautiful sister in her day, she's still a beautiful sister.

"Herb?"

"Yeah, Moms?'

"Listen to me close. I'm not gon' repeat myself."

He remoted the sound down without taking his eyes from his mother's face.

"It's hard out there for a young Black man. We all know that. You just got out of jail which is gonna make things a little bit harder, but I don't want you to give up on yourself. O.K.?"

"O.K. Moms . . . with you in my corner I know everything is gon' be awright.

"Good, now turn it up a little and let's hear what Oprah is talking about today."

*   *   *

They both reacted with pleased expressions to see each other on the Blue Line again.

"Hey, how you doing?! You still spilling stuff all over the place?"

The bell toned laughter unsettled he was so close to it.

"Ohhh noooo, I'm O.K. now. It's just that I was sooo sleepy that day. I had been studying for my exams and you know, with this other job, I was . . . how you say .. exhaustedly."

It was his turn to laugh. "Exhaustedly." She means "exhausted." A cute lil' accent . . .

"So what's up? I mean, you know, what do you do?"

Five minutes later, he felt "exhaustedly" from listening to her describe her six day grind of student nurse's aide studies—part time waitress regime.

"Wowww! You be doin' a lotta stuff, huh?"

She nodded her head in agreement. This guy really understands what I'm going through.

They continued chatting, with long pause lines in between spurts of conversation.

"So, you say you from Nicaragua? That's near Brazil, right?"

"0 no, eets en Central America."

"Now I gotcha, its between North America and South America."

"Well, almost like that, eets below Mexico."

Herb felt at ease talking to this young woman from Nicaragua. She's about taking care of business, I like that.

She nodded with her chin to the exit as the train slowed to her stop.

"This is my place."

"When will I see you again?," he asked impulsively. She look stunned for a moment and then lowered her eyelashes as she answered.

"I am riding the Blue Line about this time almost every day."

"Well, I'll see you then . . . ."

She raised her eyelashes and gave him a curious look but didn't say anything. Herb felt a moment of desperation as the train came to a stop.

"Uhh, what's your name?"

"Blanca, Blanca Cruz Somoza."

"I'm Herb Finley."

She barely touched his outstretched hand and fled to the exit. Passing his window on the station platform, she responded to his off-eye wink with a shy sprinkling of her fingers.

About this time . . . uhh huh.

Herb spent the rest of the week going from one job interview to another.

"Now then, Mr. Finley, you state here on your application that you are on parole?"

"I'm on parole, yes, but I didn't commit any crime, I was framed!"

"Oh, I see . . . ."

About this time almost every day . . . .

He raced from his last job interview to take the train he thought she would be on. He rode from one station to another, got off the train, rode back the other way for three station stops and repeated his actions.

About this time almost every day, huh?

"Herb, you got a call from this computer training center, man named Steiner, wants you to call him back."

"Heyyy, that's the one I told you about, remember, who said young men make mistakes . . . ."

"I got my fingers crossed and I'm goin' to say a prayer or two for you."

"Thanks, Moms, I need all the help I can get."

Two weeks later Herb Finley was a member of Class Two Thousand, a test group of young people of several ethnic backgrounds who had been chosen to participate in a pilot work—study program.

"Mom, it's the Bomb! You hear me, it's the Bomb!"

"I knew you could do it, Herby, I knew you could do it!"

He saw the reflection of her face in the train window as she sat beside him, loaded with notebooks and folders.

"Hey, Blancha . . ."

"No, eets Blanca".

"That's what I mean, how you been? I thought I had missed you."

"I've seen you two, three times but you were there and I was here and the train was going, you know."

"So, how you been? I just got a gig in a program. Things is looking good for me. Real good . . ."

She looked at him with real interest for the first time.

Nice guy, he's so enthusiastic about life.

"Blancha. 0 sorry, Blanca, I'm just runnin' off at the mouth. I haven't given you a chance to say nothin . . . ." That Mexican couple there, why are they giving us the stink eye?

"I have nothing to say . . . ."

They looked out of the window at the familiar scenery for a few beats, before Herb could jack up the courage to speak again. He spoke in a low voice, almost as though he were doing a monologue.

"Look, I know I'm a stranger and all that, but I'm a nice guy, I got friends who'll testify to that.

"I'm not the kind of dude who chases after girls all the time and stuff like that. As a matter of fact, I don't even have a girlfriend.

"I don't know what your situation is 'cause I didn't want to get into your business 'n stuff . . . ."

Blanca nodded quietly, to indicate that she too was unattached.

"Actually, all I'm saying is that it would be nice to have a real conversation with you, you know when we're not on the train. Maybe we could . . . uhh . . . stop off and get a hamburger and a coke or something . . . ."

She took careful note of the small beads of sweat that ringed Herb's forehead, and clinically recorded the phenomenon as a result of nervous agitation. Her station was next.

"Yes, maybe we could have a conversation?"

This is America and I'm twenty-three years old. I shouldn't have to have Mama and Papa approve of every action I make. What did they say when Roberto came home with the Jewish girl? Nada. They looked at each other, but no one said anything.

The train was sliding to a stop.

"Well, uhh, when? I mean, you got a number? I can call you."

She stood at the edge of the seat, lurching a bit as the train ground to a stop.

"I'm riding the Blue Line about this time almost every day."

The big smile she gave him destroyed his developing protests.

"I'm looking forward to seeing you, O.K.?"

"Yes, I also," she answered boldly, surprising both of them.

Herb was tempted to escort her to the exit, but held himself in check. That wouldn't be cool. No that wouldn't be cool at all.

On the platform she turned to pantomime—see you—and blew a very shy kiss to him from the tips of her fingers.

Herb stared at the gesture, his lower jaw open with delight and surprise. "Wowww!"

He made careful note of the time frame and the station. I'm gon' really surprise her tomorrow. Think I better hit the geography book tonight and find out where Nicaragua is.

CHAPTER THREE

Donna took the last sip of her espresso, glanced at the statue mounted on the obelisk in front of the Long Beach City Hall tossed her empty cup into the trash bin on the station platform and stepped into the Los Angeles bound Blue Line train.

It took her a moment to decide where to sit. She made several considerations: It's two o'clock, the sun won't be too hot if I sit on the west side of the train and it won't get crowded until we get to Compton.

She stared out of the train window, thinking of Katie.

"0, you didn't drive? I'll take you home."

"No problem, the Blue Line is cool, it gives me a chance to mingle with the people."

"I guess that's the social activist in you. I try to avoid 'the people' as much as I can, especially these days."

"Why?"

"They're dangerous, haven't you heard?"

She smiled, thinking back to her —"Let's do lunch Thursday" – with her sorority sister, Kate Adams-Johnson.

"I've thought about asking Frank to change his name a half dozen times. What could sound more common than Adams-Johnson?"

Kate was always fun to share a few hours with, take in a show, have lunch at one of the upscale places on 3rd and Pine, drink a couple glasses of wine, discuss their lives.

"So how does it feel to be past the change?"

"You tell me, sister you went first."

They could joke with each other like sisters, share memories from their college days and beyond.

"Donna, if anyone had ever tried to force me to believe that you and Fred would ever divorce . . ."

"I know, it seems unreal to me too, but you know how it is with a lot of men when they start feeling old. They'll do anything to fight off the inevitable. I think, for most of them, that they see a younger woman as a testimonial of their youth or something."

"Well, I'm not having any of that out of Mr. Johnson; I've served firm notice."

Donna closed her eyes and tilted her face slightly to catch the sun.

Girlfriends. There used to be six of us, now there's only two of us, a little older, a little wiser, a little heavier. She and Kate took pride in being "fifty some years old" with firm waistlines and no double chins.

"I think it's stupid to be running around with your thighs rubbing together, don't you?"

Donna Hightower opened her eyes as the train lurched into motion and looked at her reflection in the window. You're right, Kate, you're right.

Riding the Blue Line was a bit like sight-seeing for her.

She never felt bored by the trip from Long Beach to Slauson, always something to see, a story to watch.

"Donna, you ought to be a writer, you know that. You see stories everywhere you go." That's what her ex-husband used to tell her.

She studied the faces and postures of the people who got on and off the train. God, some of the ugliest people are making some of the most beautiful babies. Beautiful babies.

Uncouth teenagers who talk as though their mouths were sewers and prop their feet on the seats.

Well, how can you blame them for the way they act, no home training. My parents would have killed me before they would allow me to behave like that.

Hmmmmm . . . not as many crazies as they have on the busses.

It goes to show you what can be done by adding a few policemen making some serious rules.

Her heart swelled into her throat when the man stepped into the train. He strolled up the aisle and sat in a seat on the opposite side of the aisle, diagonally from hers.

She made an oblique study of his profile, feeling a quick rush of heat dampen her temples. Am I having hot flashes, or is it him?

Jim Brown, the man who "made the earth move" for her, twenty-five short years ago.

He looks good, just about the way I would expect him to look today. She took careful note of the trim waistline.

"Don't you just hate these middle-aged men who look like they're pregnant?!"

"Now be nicer Kate, we have a lot of women running around here, looking like they're pregnant too."

"Yeahhh, but they have a right to look that way—they have been pregnant."

The firm chin, that gray at the temples, the serious expression I always loved. Did I love him."

The man in the seat next to her stood up to exit. Donna leaned across the aisle to tap Jim Brown on the shoulder, panicking for a moment at the idea that she might be mistaken.

"There's a vacancy here, mister," she said with a seductive smile. She took the turn he made toward her, and the joy of his expression, in slow motion.

"Donna!! Donna!! I don't believe this!"

The people who turned to stare at the couple, returned to reading their books, newspapers and staring out of the window when they realized that they were not witnessing a fight.

He held her at arm's length after a long, fervent hug and an ardent kiss that landed dangerously close to her mouth.

"This is unbelievable! I was just thinking about you yesterday, as a matter of fact."

"And what, pray tell, were you thinking?"

He squeezed her hand, "Same ol' Donna, right on the point. You haven't changed at all."

"Are you serious?" Are you saying you don't think I've changed since you left me to go do your thing in Washington, D.C.?"

"I didn't leave you, Donna. I hate to hear you put it like that."

"How would you put it?"

The euphoric bounce of their meeting again on the Blue Line in Los Angeles after twenty-five years, suddenly did a spiral. She could feel it.

"I think it was a matter of misplaced priorities, now that I look back at it. I thought the position I was going to take in Washington, D.C. was going to be more important then . . . ."

"More important than me?"

The train slid to a stop, disgorged passengers and sucked others in before he answered!

"Yes, to be honest about it. But you have to remember that you had told me a half dozen times that you weren't ready for a full fledged commitment. Remember?"

The train was a little more crowded, a few more stroller clogged the entrance/exit. Three more stations.

"And so, you got married too."

"I needed someone."

He said the words with so much feeling she wanted to put her arms around him and tell him . . ."Yes, I understand."

"And you got married too."

She nodded yes.

"And I've been divorced for five years now. And you?"

"She died two years ago, lung cancer. She just couldn't stop puffing.

The train seemed to be flying through space for a few moments. They were engulfed by silence, despite the fact that they were surrounded by people making all kinds of noises.

"Sorry to hear about that . . . her. I really am. Well, this is my stop coming up."

He stood to exit with her, brushing past the people boarding the train.

"You transferring here too?"

"No, I'm getting off to talk to you."

They stood on the high platform at Slauson, staring into each other's faces as though they had experienced a miracle.

"You know I never expected to see you again. Am I making you late for something?"

"No, well, I've got an appointment downtown and I'll be late, but it doesn't matter, they can't do it 'til I get there."

They exchanged understanding smiles. Still in control, huh?

"Can I call you? Maybe we could have dinner together? Maybe this evening?"

She broadened her smile. Same ol' Jim, always ready for action.

"Are you sure you want to see me again? Remember, I'm the same ol' Donna, I haven't changed . . . ."

"I hope so".

He opened his arms to embrace her as the horn sounded, announcing that his train had arrived.

*   *   *

Siren on the Metro Bus (Transfer) . . .

Even on a crowded bus in would've been very hard to ignore Darrilyn. It had something to do with the warm aura that seemed to halo her graceful movements.

She was not tall but she seemed to be. She was not classically beautiful by anybody's standard, but she was gorgeously seductive. Her appeal was inter-denominational, international, wholistic.

The Asians saw her as an Asian, the African-Americans saw her as Black, the Latinos saw her as one of them and the Whites took her at face value. Her basic appeal was to men, but there were also a number of women who found themselves orbiting in her atmosphere.

Darrilyn rode the Wilshire Blvd. bus, east and west, at least twice a day, a complete boomerang.

Perhaps she was going somewhere or maybe she wasn't. She was definitely leaving a string of illusioned men (and women) in her wake.

She had an artless technique that was constructed by having eye to eye contact with the one she had chosen. But she could also carry off the same business with a swanish turn of her head, or by channeling charged emotions into the languid movement of a flexible wrist or into a heaven blessed smile.

She carried business cards that identified her as a professional astrologer—"See the stars with Darrilyn." And from time to time she placed one of her cards in the hands of a prospective "client." A number of men were pleasantly surprised by her card, a few were honestly bewildered, but no one was ever known to refuse to accept her offering.

This was taking place within the Los Angeles bus system. The Metropolitan Transportation Authority, a gulag that closely resembled all of the other large city bus-gulag-systems, reflecting the fast forward insanity of large city-living on wheels.

Cliques of criminally insane people ride the bus, grinding their mad teeth, slobbering, arguing with invisible foes, threatening to blow themselves up and everything around them, dynamite heads.

Molesters of all types: child, animal, plant, environment.

Crazy people with no criminal intentions whatsoever, bring their lice spliced blankets, their unwashed bodies and their ragged, greasy slimy clothes on board.

They also talk to invisible beings. Men step on dressed as women, women as men, in between types cross-dress.

People sit in configured seats, nursing grudges from past centuries. People sit next to each other, weeping from internal pains that have become exquisite.

Old people think thoughts of times and places that are as distant and foreign as the moon. Young people speak and act in ways that are so incomprehensible to the old people that they blot them out of their conscious minds.

Foreigners, all are foreigners, speak about life on the bus, on Earth in America, as though it were unlike anything they've ever known. They can't believe that so many bad spirited people could be in one place at the same time.

No doubt about it, the bus functions as a spaceship on the ground, filled with spaced out Earthlings, Darrilyn is just one of them.

"Uhhh, excuse me please, is this seat taken?"

The tall Mexican man with the Pedro Armendariz eyes and mustache, who gave every sign to indicate that he thought of himself as a "ladies man," stared at the voluptuous creature leaning toward him.

The bus is half empty and she wants to sit next to me, this beautiful woman. I am truly blessed today.

He managed to perform a gracious bullfighter's media Veronica while seated. Darrilyn slid into the vacant seat, trailing diaphanous scarves and Chanel No. 5.

The bus, staggering from stop to stop, had become a sports car, flitting from block to block. The man felt heat rush from the follicles in his scalp down to the bottleneck in his bikini briefs. Ahhhh, this one, what can I say to her?

"I must introduce myself, I am Juan Carlos Fuerte."

"And I am Darrilyn."

She placed her hand in his and caressed it with a shake. Juan Carlos Fuerte burned a hole in her face with his eyes. This is the woman of my dreams.

She looks Spanish, not Mexican, Spanish. Or maybe Argentine. Does she speak Spanish?

"Do you speak Spanish?"

"Only enough to get me in trouble."

Their faces glowed with smiles for each other. The man was certain that he had fallen in love with the woman. And vice versa. It was there for all to see.

"Then, we will have to say what has to be said in Inglés," he said in a passion driven, husky whisper.

"Yes, I suppose so", she replied, lowering her voice to match his, and folded her hands between her thighs as though she were in church. The graceful folding of her hands and the placement almost caused Juan Carlos Fuerte to speak Spanish.

"You know you are a very beautiful woman."

He felt her melt into the seat beside him, his words had done it. He felt the urge to use many, many words, to overwhelm this gorgeous creature with words and then jump off of the bus, transfer and go to this nice little room his friend had in East Los Angeles.

"Everything about you excites me, your perfume, your clothes, the way you are, everything . . . ."

"Juan, you say the most beautiful things to me, I've never heard anyone talk like this before.

He stroked his mustache and gently reached between her thighs to grasp both of her hands in his hands.

"Maybe you have never heard these things before because we have never met before. Darrrilina . . ."

"Darrilyn, my name is Darrilyn."

"Ah, yes, Darrilyn, the woman who has come to me out of a dream . . . ."

He slipped his arm to the cusp of her shoulders and immediately withdrew it. I mustn't let one of Maria's nosy friends catch me. Darrilyn gave him an oblique, coy look.

"Darrilyn, listen, I have a wonderful idea."

"Yes?"

She seemed so eager to share his feelings, so reasonable, so honest, so . . . sexy.

"Why don't we go somewhere together, me, you, just the two of us?"

She answered him with the same sense of urgency in her voice.

"Where? Where would you like to go with me, Juan?"

She's a woman, she's not a girl. She doesn't act like a girl, but she doesn't really make me feel like she's a loose thing either. I'll take a chance, I'll speak my mind.

"Uhhh, I was thinking we could go to this place; it's like a friend's house, you know? It's not too far from here." There were no other passengers on the bus now. They had all been bubbled out, forgotten, dismissed.

The speeding sports car had jetted to a halt, waiting for the green light words to speed it off again. Darrilyn gently pulled her hands out of Juan's smoky clutches.

"Juan, as much as I would like to, I can't go with you . . . ."

He held himself in check for a full beat, listening for "because." It never came. She simply stopped at "I can't go with you . . . ."

"May I ask why?" he asked, and wedged himself closer to her. She turned toward him with a bright, feverish look in her eyes.

"I'm a professional astrologer."

Juan cocked his head to one side, deeply interested in whatever this fascinating woman had to say. But what did astrology have to do with what he was suggesting? "A professional astrologer, huh?"

"Yes."

Fifteen minutes later he felt that he had some idea what a professional astrologer was, and what they were responsible for doing.

"So you see, that's why I can't go with you. Here is my card. Please call me, I may have some important information for you."

Darrilyn stood quickly, sprinkled a little wave goodbye and popped out of the exit doors like an exploding Jack-in-the-Box.

Juan Carlos Fuerte, frustrated Lothario, stared at the plain white card. The name Darrilyn was printed in bold black face, her title "Professional Astrologer" and a telephone number.

He looked out of the window to catch a last glimpse of the enchanting creature he had just met, but she was nowhere to be seen.

*　　*　　*

The man could have been any one of the thousands of grey headed, grey bearded, middle aged African American men who were forced to take the bus to wherever they were going that morning.

It was more than obvious, from the subconsciously developed frown on his nutbrown face that he was pissed off: he was pissed at his prostate, the amount of sleep he was losing every night being forced to piss. He was pissed with his colon, and the need to have it examined once a year.

He was pissed at the idea of needing glasses to read the small print, at the heartburn he suffered from, at the stiffness in his joints and the consortium of pills he had to take for regular ailments. But above all, he was pissed because he couldn't flirt with young women any more.

They seemed to be amused, rather than attracted, to his eye winks, his macho posturing and his baritone inquiries. And when the young ladies that he had an eye for were not amused they seemed to be terrified. He had come to the conclusion that most of the women who rode the bus, under thirty, had probably been molested by an older man.

He was pissed off about that, about the lousy vibe these other dirty old men had released in generations of nubile females.

He had some of these things on his mind, including concerns about his bills, when Darrilyn winked at him from across the aisle.

Maybe there's something in her eye. No, that's not it, she's winking at me. Myron Smith took a deep breath and turned to see if he could catch the reflection in the bus window of the young woman who looked at him.

Yes, he could see her in the mirror-window. He studied the reflection for a few beats. Fine young woman. One of those multicolored women, and she's definitely checking me out.

The large woman sharing Darrilyn's seat stood, swayed with the bus lurching to a stop and stumbled to the exit.

Myron hesitated for a beat or two before he slid into the empty seat beside Darrilyn.

They exchanged warm, opaque smiles. Darrilyn turned to stare out of the window, Myron Smith stared at her profile.

So nice when you have people who don't act like they're scared to death of other people.

"Beautiful day, isn't it?" he asked, allowing the words to flow like baritoned honey. He liked the sound of his voice and knew how to use it.

"Ohhh, it's just gorgeous!"

He was pleasantly stunned by Darrilyn's ebullience.

"Uhhh, yeahhh, you're right, it really is."

They both stared out of the window as though they were looking at a picture, glittering in the smog of mid day Los Angeles. Myron felt the blood rush to his head. He couldn't tell if it was from the excitement of chatting with an attractive young woman or if his high blood pressure was acting up.

Damn, did I take my pills?

He fumbled into the pocket of his cotton windbreaker for his high blood pressure pills, unscrewed the top and dry swallowed a pill.

"You O.K.?," she asked, taking note of his actions.

"Awwww, I'm O.K., just some ol' pills I have to take every now and then."

Her smile was so warm, so concerned, so sweet.

"Isn't that wonderful that all we have to do is take a pill every now and then to stay well? 0, incidentally, I'm Darrilyn."

He was pleased with the firm grip of her handshake. He hated to shake hands with women, especially the ones who touched hands as though they were handling five day old fish.

"And I'm Myron Smith. So, where you going on this gorgeous day?"

"Where? O, just anywhere. I just want to drift! To go with the flow!"

"Why don't you have a cup of coff . . . , uhh, espresso with me?"

"I'd love to."

Myron felt like hugging Darrilyn, but resisted the urge.

She'll think I'm just another dirty ol' man. And the V.A. appointment? What the hell, I'll reschedule. Ain't nothing for me to do but stay Black 'n die, may as well have a lil' fun in my life before I go out.

The Gourmet Coffee House was a place that he would never have gone to by himself.

A student hangout, south of the University, filled with students pontificating, staring at their laptops, acting romantic, being young.

"How did you know about this place?"

"0, I come here all the time."

He swallowed hard, checking out the coffee prices. Damn! What the hell do they put in this stuff anyway? 0 well, there goes my beer money for this month.

"Myron, you know we can go Dutch on this."

"Darrilyn, I invited you for coffee. This is my treat, now. Order what you like."

He thought he detected snide looks peeking out at them from behind a couple of the bearded faces. Probably think I'm a sugar daddy, huh?

He smiled at the idea. What kind of sugar could this daddy come up with, on a fixed income?

They ordered, espresso double for him, café latte for her, and began to talk as though they were old friends who happened to run into each other on the bus.

Myron Smith stared at Darrilyn as she spoke, focusing on the ideas that she spilled out to him.

"I'm a professional astrologer."

"Oh, you spend a lot of time star gazing, huh?"

"No, that's an astronomer. I'm an astrologer."

"0, I see said the blind man . . ." He loved the expression that brightened her face as she quickly realized what he had said.

"That's pretty witty, Mr. Smith, preeety witty."

"Please, call me Myron."

She squeezed his forearm with real affection, boosting his ego yea high. He couldn't think of anything else to say to her. What words could he use to tell her that he loved her? That he had felt love for her the moment he saw her? How to say . . . ?

"Please, Myron, don't say anything."

He was startled by her intuitive reading. Yes, this is that special one I've been looking for, since Mabel's death.

Darrilyn stood, and indicated with gestures that she was off to the ladies room. He nodded pleasantly and watched her stride away from their table.

Mmmmmmmm . . . that's a fine woman there, a real fine woman.

He sipped his espresso and smiled to himself . . . you ol' rogue, you. Here you are, three years older 'n black pepper and got the nerve to be seducing pretty young things off the bus. What's gonna become of you?

He crossed his legs at the knee and began to try to put together "a program." I'll invite her over for dinner tomorrow evening. Bet that would ring her bell. Ain't too many young men who know how to cook these days and most of the young women can't even boil water.

I wonder if she can cook? Well, we don't have to worry about that. I can cook.

A blurred succession of image/thoughts slipped through his mind; Darrilyn and Myron at the movies, taking a long walk on a moonblanched beach, sharing laughs, making love. He glanced around him, checking people out, as though someone might have read his thoughts.

Making love. He uncrossed his knees and sprawled back in his seat. Making love. I haven't made love to a woman in two years, since Mabel died. Making love. Well, I really can't count Ernestine. She was just doing what she thought old friends should do. Helping me to get past my grief, I guess you could say.

He did a surreptitious tummy tuck with his left hand. She doesn't seem to mind this age thing. Some women are like that, they're able to see past the superficial stuff. What's age got to do with emotional involvement anyway?

"Are you Smith?"

"Huhh?

"Are you named Smith?"

He felt a bit awkward about being caught daydreaming by their waitress. She'll probably think I'm senile or something.

"Yeah, yeah, I'm Smith."

The waitress handed him a small square sheet of paper, folded neatly in half, and strolled off to attend another table.

"Dear Myron, it's been truly wonderful, but I had to continue with the flow. Please call me sometime. Universely yours, Darrilyn."

He turned the piece of paper over frantically, looking for a telephone number. She hadn't written one. Myron Smith settled back in his seat and stared at the people rushing past the picture window of the Gourmet Coffee House, trying to center his shattered feelings. A few moments later, after putting it all into a perspective that he felt comfortable with, he signaled to the waitress for the check.

"The bill has already been paid, sir."

He stood and shook the kink out of his left leg, a big smile on his face, and slowly walked out of the coffee house.

Well, what the hell, you win some, you lose some. Better to have a few of these kinds of times than not have any at all. Maybe I'll run into her again.

CHAPTER FOUR

Koreatown . . .

Master Kim felt completely bewildered by the actions and activities of the people on the bus, but he didn't allow his feelings to show.

The young White couple at the back of the bus, kissing and feeling on each other. The shame he felt about their conduct was transmitted to the other Koreans on the bus, who informed him with a glance . . . this is not Korea, this is America, this is the way they are.

Master Kim bowed his head in thought. Riding the bus for a month was his idea.

I want to get to know the people. In Korea there are only Koreans; here there are many different kinds of people. When I open the doors of my dojang and they come, I must know who they are, how they are, what they think.

I have never had a conversation with a Mexican, a Black, Filipino . . . . I must know them, they will be coming to Tosan dojang.

Master Kim's relatives and those friends who had been in Los Angeles for years before he decided to see "this America," simply smiled and bowed.

One could not tell an 8th Dan in their national martial art form, Tae Kwon Do, what to do, and how to do it. They all bowed discreetly and offered their advice concerning the different kinds of people he would be likely to meet.

No one could possibly prepare him for the madness that he was likely to experience during the course of his one month trip around town.

Daily he set out from his apartment in Koreatown to ride the buses. Sometimes (using his monthly bus pass) he rode the Wilshire bus west as far as it would go, or east. And the Vermont bus south, as far as it would go. Or the Western Avenue bus. Or one of the others.

It took a full week of being constantly shocked by the anti—social behavior of the people for him to relax; why did the people rush and push each other to board the bus? Why did they frown so much? Why were the people so . . . so isolated from each other?

Why did the young African-American men, good potential for Tae Kwo Do, disrespect everyone so badly?

One afternoon, on the westbound bus to Venice, two Black men, maybe fifteen-sixteen years old, screamed dirty words, pounded on the seats in the back of the bus, told obscene stories to each other, obviously begging others to listen in on their misery. Master Kim felt like crying. What kind of pain would produce people to behave in such a fashion?

He made a special effort to listen to them, to try to understand what was forcing them to misbehave so badly.

Why would they put their shoes onto the seats that other people would be sitting in?

They had no respect for others. They had no respect for themselves. He wasn't gang-sophisticated enough to determine if they were doing what they were doing because they had to, or because they had been driven to that nebulous nihilism that spells self-destruction.

I must work on the African-American youth . . . . I must teach them to control their anger.

The straight-out crazies were much more complicated for him to relate to. First off, Master Kim's English language skills were not way up there, and many of the English warbling crazies could sometimes ensnare him, emotionally, with their convoluted, psycho-Babylonized-mush chat, before he realized where they were.

He "talked" to one poor, homeless, obese, drastically sexually abused African-American teenager (maybe) for fifteen consecutive bus stops before he realized that the youngster needed more help than he could possibly offer.

The types of madnesses running around freely distressed and disturbed him. How can they allow people who are completely crazy to ride the bus?

The clothes, the tattoos, the craziness made him feel very sad, but the attitudes of the people made him feel even worse. Some were "normal" people who could see the bright side of life, but most seemed to be bogged down by personal demons . . . .

*   *   *

Maybe he was ready for Darrilyn when she came.

"Good morning, Sir."

The brightness of the greeting, the open flavor of the woman's voice startled him.

"Ahhh, good morning."

They rode side by side, exchanging obliquely pleasant smiles. Master Kim was intrigued by the young woman's attitude-vibe.

She is obviously someone who has a healthy regard for herself. Master Kim decided to make an effort to use his whiplash English.

"This is nice day, you think?"

"0 yes, certainly. Any day that gives us an opportunity to begin breathing is a nice day, to put it mildly."

Master Kim puzzled over the flow of her words and came to the conclusion that she was saying something he agreed with.

"My English, you know, not good."

"Ohhh, don't worry about it," she announced in high gliding tones. "This is America, no one speaks good English here."

He nodded to her, a smile creasing his face. This is a nice person.

"Where going?" he asked, feeling more confidence in his language skills.

"It could be here. It could be there. I'm just riding. And what about you, where are you going?"

"I am also here and also there."

They laughed aloud at the joke they shared and shook hands. Master Kim felt a certain kind of awkwardness, shaking a woman's hand, especially one who was younger than himself, but in America, do as the Americans.

Block after block they talked, exchanging ideas, points of view. He was delighted to know that she knew something about Tae Kwon Do.

"Hand and foot way, a very interesting way to look at the world. I have had several clients who studied this art."

"And you, the astro-logist, I like this also."

Language was left far behind their relationship to each other. They could feel that, the people around them could feel the vibe,

Master Kim studied the woman's hands, her feet, the beauty of her neck and ears, the positive way she sat in her seat.

She was the first woman from another race that he had ever felt attracted to. But she seemed so Asian. Perhaps one of her parents was an Asian.

"Well, this is where I get off."

He stared at her, stunned by her declaration.

"Here, you are getting off."

"Yes," she answered him and moved quickly to the exit.

Master Kim felt like leaving the bus with her, but he had not been invited and he didn't want to lose face. He looked at her as she stood at the exit door, waiting for the bus to stop, wishing that he could invent a reason for being with her a little longer.

She dipped into her Kente cloth bag and pulled out a card as they shuddered to a halt

"Here, this is my card. Get in touch with me if you wanna have your chart done."

He studied the name for a few seconds, to familiarize himself with the sound, and bowed in her direction. Darrilyn was gone.

*　*　*

A Brief Nap—

Click On: "Bone Daddy's Journey"

How did it begin? Well, to be gloriously honest with you, I don't know. That is to say, I don't know how it began, but I do know when it began. It began in nineteen hundred 'n 88.

In nineteen hundred 'n 88, in search of Heaven inspired rhythms, the elusive sound of the bluest chord ever played, and a woman named Self-Determination (the Nguzo Saba has the key to this translation-code), I flew nervously to Oakland.

All might have been cool if I had only subleased my apartment. Mr. and Mrs. Chan, after ten years of hard Berimbau listening, would have granted my every wish. I was still paying the lowest rent for a trendy area apartment, solely on the basis of me being "Bone Daddy."

"0, please don't worry about prosaic stuff, you are destined to pay us the six months back rent soon. Go about your business, we are not worried about you."

That's the way it was between me and my landlords. Could anything be better? I mean, when you have that sort of understanding between you and your landlord . . . Hello!

If only I had subleased that beautifully designed, gorgeously situated, one bedroom palace when the Frenzies drove me to fly to Oakland. But I didn't, I gave it up.

I invited Tabula, Donna, Cedric, Synthia St. James (subsequently famous for designing a U.S. postage stamp), Waheed, 'Bridge, Henrique, Eliana, D.J., Willie, Nancy Cox, Amde, Richard and Otis (the Persuasions of the poetic world) and hundreds of other well meaning spirits to share my "going out."

Bottom line: I gave up my apartment. Never more would my sexually conservative neighbors (Italians who screamed "fuck you" out of their second floor windows at each other, next door Armenian, Chinese puritans) have to redface me the next day, after listening, horrified, no doubt, to the screams of histrionically inclined African-Americans. Or wonder what the hell I had done with the trio of Brazilian sisters who had done a midnight session with me. And followed me, loaded on cachasah and empadao, to continue the play.

Nor would I have to subtly subtitle for the Chans, my landlord friends, after evenings filled with music from the Corrida, female circumcision ceremonies, Afro-Cuban Santeria rites and the blues from a few brothers who had paid their dues in Angola (not the country, the prison in Louisiana).

Gave it up. Never thought I'd have any need for the place anymore after Self-Determination.

We were going to call it, "This Time."

What it spelled out was quite clear to me. I, "Bone Daddy," had declared an end to my boning. That's how highly I thought of Self-Determination. And still do. Ase.

The chords, red and blue, and some that I would never be able to describe were there. The Heaven inspired rhythms were there. Some of them resembled earthquakes ("and did the Earth move for you, Bone Daddy?"). But a lot of other goodies were blocked by Self-Determination's self-righteous rigidity and brutal insensitivity. The danger zone was curved.

None of these qualities were apparent to me when I made myself apartmentless and flew nervously to Oakland. It took months to discover the cause of my night sweats, why my molars were grinding themselves to nubs, why my stomach was churning before and after the Heaven inspired rhythms had played out.

It didn't matter to her, these feelings, for her, the control freak, all that really mattered was that I obey the will of self-determined Self-Determination.

Little bit like a religious fanatic who asks very few questions but has all the answers. I felt trapped. The boning was tres bon, no doubt about that, but there are times when even the tres bon of boning won't cover up for what's bad. I began to plot my escape.

Most of the exits were barricaded with sex-furniture, promises, visions, sinsemilla reasoning, concepts that meant a lot, even if they weren't carried out to the letter.

We wanted "This Time" to be the real time, we really did. We were both seasoned vets of the emotional wars, with hundreds of wounds (and wounded) in our files and felt a serious need to have "This Time" be "The Time."

For two long hill dipping years we tried. The bookies in Oakland libeled me a dark horse, maybe the darkest, and pushed the odds up to a hundred to one against the dark horse limping across the finish line.

Kahlil Gibran, the Lebanese mystic, is the one who wrote, "We should love what is between us, not each other." Well, that might've been good advice for a lot of lovers, but for me and Self-Determination, there was too much between us.

I doubt if I spent one whole week without staring into the abscessed eyes of one of her ex-men; they were everywhere. Well, I guess that was to be expected. After all, I had moved onto her turf. I was between them and her.

Frequently, I scrapped my escape plan because the music had been exceptionally groovy that night (morning, afternoon, mid-afternoon, evening, mid-evening, dawn, midnight, whenever we got into the groove) and I just couldn't see myself straying too far from the magic of her music.

Frequently, my escape plans were foiled by the deeply felt circumnavigations of the self-determined head. There were moments when I could almost say that she held me captive by the powers of her mind, head.

Matters finally came to a head, I guess I could say, on a trip we made to a conference in the San Bernardino mountains. After the conference, on the way down, appropriately, I made an instant decision.

"Drop me at my friend's house in Torrance."

"You're not going back with me?"

"No."

So, there I was in Torrance with $75 and the clothes on my back. I was free. Free of the delicious tortures inflicted deliberately (and accidentally), free of the tyranny of a love that was too tough, bent, warped and shaped by previous investors.

My whole body felt that it was being pulled, magnetized to her cherry red vehicle as it shot away from the curb, and at the same time, absurdly, a weight was suddenly lifted from my head.

I spent the next two years living in my friend's garage, sleeping on a mattress that was piled on layers of cardboard and newspapers. "Bone Daddy's nest," one of my girlfriends called it.

Of course, I had to trip back and forth to Oakland a few times to grab a couple leftover boxes and have my pleasure pan singed. So much danger, so much. I was never certain that I was going to be able to escape again, until the last second.

But I did pull away, the cruel thoughts of what I had endured shot me straight back to Torrance.

From 1990 to 1992, I wrote books and I read books. I will never be able to say how many books I wrote or read. There were evenings, during the rainy season, with the droplets on the roof sounding like Tito Puente, when I wrote two 500 hundred page novels. Two . . .

My dream time was unaltered, left intact. My friend didn't really care what I was doing in the garage, and I didn't really care what he was doing in the house. We came together for conversations and to watch one of his favorite t.v. shows in the evening.

(Never could figure out what was supposed to be so appetizing about "The Love Connection." But, hey, what do I know?)

I felt like a special kind of Monk; maybe I had drifted away from the Major Vehicle to something that might be called a "garage monk," definitely an offshoot of one of the major sects.

During the course of the day, my friend at work, with no one to distract my focus, I did five things.

I walked about a mile (of long, long Torrance auto-designed blocks) to this huge, neighborhood park for my morning Capoeira workout.

Capoeira workout. What's that? Stretching, moving, kicking, sweating for an hour. Home, with the good jelly feeling in your upper body, the tight urge to kick in the legs. Home for a ritual shower, hot and then cold.

Write. I would write about what I was writing, write what I was writing, write what I was going to write. Write.

Read. Once a week I staged a guerilla raid on the Torrance Library and came away with treasures that they didn't know they had.

"A Survey of African Dances? Are you sure we have that?"

"About 92 percent, seems likely that someone has written something like that. Check your computer."

And, after surveying/reading as much as I could possibly read about the dances of Africa, I would write some more. Some of this writing may have been very good, I don't know. I simply wrote and let whatever was going to happen to it happen.

Some of it got published, some of it didn't get published. Some of it I'm still writing . . . .

In the garage, I sometimes spent days sprawled on "Bone Daddy's Nest," staring up at the gorgeous spider webs that emblazoned the garage ceiling. I spent days not moving my lips, other then to say "Hello" and/or "Goodbye."

I would be pushing the envelope (uugghh, hate that term) to suggest that this was a deliberate thing. I think it was simply about what it was about. There was no one to talk to or anybody to talk about somebody with. So why talk?

(Real fast forward, Sat at Lake Merritt, in Oakland, California, this past Wednesday, June 5, 1998, talking with my friend, Lena Slachmuijlder, who had just pulled in from Accra, Ghana.

She was giving me loads of help to try to help Grace Appiah, the woman I love, to secure a visa.)

As we talked, Ishmael Reed strolled past. He may have been exercising in his exercise clothes. No telling. Ishmael is a strange dude. He looked at me and recognized me, and I looked at him and recognized him. We exchanged salutes—"Uhh-ugh." Or something like that.

Lena didn't know who he was and I couldn't immediately think up enough titles to explain to her why he is considered "an important Black writer." I wouldn't've been able to explain why he was important. Or considered Black. Or a writer (by some, in any case).

It had something to do with what went through me on a daily basis in my friend's garage. It wasn't an easy time, those two years. I don't know if Africa was calling me before I moved into the garage, or if Self-Determination had intercepted the previous phonings.

In another man's garage the call became quite insistent. Africa was calling me. Specifically, Ghana, West Africa. The drumming (why was I always playing somebody's conga, or buying one or two? Or going to worship Armando Peraza, Mongo Santamaria, Carlos "Patato" Valdez, Julito Collazo, Modesto Duran, Papito, Francisco Aquabella, Totico and all the others?). The sounds of the languages they speak has always been clear to me despite a serious effort to prevent us from relating to, learning about or knowing Africa. The first time I heard a prayer in Yoruba, the hair stood up on the back of my neck, and then my head. The Ga took me straight to about six centuries of Jazz that I'd never understood.

I could easily see the separate headlines in the mainstream newspapers. "Ga, a Ghanaian language, has made Bone Daddy understand Jazz much mo' betta'."

My uncles; Africa could explain my four uncles, including Uncle Sweet Milk. And maybe offer me a linchpin clue to why my Daddy was as wild as he was, and called "Honey."

In addition to that, conglomerations of people who had gone to Africa, kept going to Africa, and who were always talking about what it was. Plus the spiritual vibes that have been shaking me out of deep sleeps all of my life.

"Come on over, the waters are swimmable."

This couple that I had known in Los Angeles were now living in a section of Accra called Osu and they had a spare bedroom. The call became a siren in the night. Yeahhh, go to Ghana, see what that's about . . . .

The couple had never been intimate friends, but we had hung out on some of the same artistic fringes, so I felt at ease. I felt I knew her a little better than I knew him, but it didn't matter a whole bunch. They were offering me a stone to step across the pond.

Never would have been able to predict the kinds of problems they were, that they were having, that he was having, that she was having, that they caused me, in a hundred years. But, before all of that would be revealed to me, I'd have to get over there.

Spiritually, I was there the minute I had made up my mind to go there. The second part of the program required me to buy a round trip ticket. It seemed to be an impossible number to pull off.

I had no money in the bank, no rich relatives, no dishonest cash flow, no lucrative hustle, just a ballpoint, some notebook paper and a $170 Veterans pension. How was I going to buy a round trip ticket to Ghana, West Africa?

The solution came to me in my third dream. Simple. Sell two well written paper back books to Holloway House Publishing Company, collect the advance and move out sharply.

And that's exactly what I did. Just one small catch to the whole business; I was leaving my "home," the garage, to vault into the unknown. Where would I wind up? On the streets of Accra?

The hell with it. In May, 1992, with the smoke from the aftermath of the Rodney King pachanga still curling up over the Basin, I looked out onto the ugly, sulfite flecked clouds and started thinking about my first African based move.

I drifted off to sleep, trying to blot out the guttural curses of the man stumbling through the house. The African—American couple who had invited me to come share their place in Osu were crazies.

Damn, I wasn't really angry with them for being who or what they were; I was angry at myself for not having the common sense to check around before I made the trip. There were at least a dozen people who could've run the scene down for me.

"Well, how long is Mr. Bone Daddy gonna live with us? I mean, like, how long are we gonna have to put up with the presence of this asshole fuckin' son-of-a-bitch?

"Huh?! Answer me, bitch."

"Now, John, please. He just got here last week . . . ."

"Are your sure?! Seems to me this motherfucker been livin' in that room for months!"

It took less than a week to realize that I had landed on the wrong side of the coin. The brother was a hostile drunk and his wife was glorified (in her mind) by her martyrdom. It was a win-win situation for them and a no win-no win situation for me.

Objectively, strangely, maybe, I found myself comparing them to gangbangers I've ridden with on the Blue Line, especially that section of the run from Florence to Compton. They were screamin' for help but they wouldn't accept help. Maybe it sounds like a contradiction, but that's the only possible description one can make of behavior that begs for correction, but awaits it in order to refuse it.

Ghana, Africa, came easily. The crazed couple came hard. From May 1992 to September 1992, I lived in their house. I drank with them. I smoked with him. I fell in love on my own.

No doubt in my mind that I was going to have to leave that crazy place. If the scene in Oakland had been infected by PMS, this scene in Ghana was infected, fueled and driven by PMS of another sort, plus malaria.

I got the malaria about one month after I arrived. Malaria, in retrospect, was like a severe form of LSD intoxication, coupled to the possibility of dying. (In recent times, I've asked myself why the people who are involved with extreme mountain climbing, "recreational budgeting" and extreme "martial arts" shouldn't get into "extreme malaria."

"Extreme malaria" would offer them all of the wonderful stuff they seem to be seeking. Hallucinations are cheap, weight loss for the fat conscious is guaranteed, "drive by rush" is definitely on the menu, plus a real good sweat plus a real good chill, plus visitations, under the hallucinogenic influences of a female mosquito, of demons.)

On the serious level, malaria is a hell. And there I was, in hell, with hell in my bloodstream. Didn't matter, about me being sick for a couple weeks, it was simply a part of the mix. He continued to get drunk, come home, rant and rave, and start the next day off like a choirboy.

(Nothing is ever all bad. I met Grace while I was living in the Nasty House . . . .)

Accra is a very difficult city to live in. It's easy to get from place to place, but difficult to find a place to live. It was a crazy time for "Bone Daddy."

I would come across a hip little place in a groovy area for a million point two cedis (a thousand two hundred dollars), get halfway into the place and wind up being outbid by the guy who was offering a million point four cedis.

It went on like that for five months. It was really a bad scene. The Nasty House couple were quite aware that I was seeking accommodations elsewhere, and why, which didn't endear me to their malevolent little twisted hearts.

"Now, don't you get out there and start tellin' people what's going on in here." This, from the Lady of the house. As though no one knew. Seems that I was the only one who didn't know, 'til too late.

Five beastly long months. Finally, in desperation, I threw all of my belongings in a couple cardboard boxes and fled to the Fair Gardens Hotel ("mosquito heaven"), right across the road from the Trade Fair Centre.

Now, I could begin to do a little bit more of what a "Bone Daddy" is supposed to do, without having obscene people peek over his shoulder.

Grace was coming to me but she hadn't fully mounted my soul yet.

Four months in a Fair Gardens Hotel "cell." A window on the west that slatted out onto a sheep grazing soccer field, a door on the eastside that opened into a dead-end corridor, a "bed" with a foam rubber mattress, a chair and a small round table, a room that held generations of female mosquitoes captive, who took out their anger on me, nightly,

Four hot months of sizzling malaria episodes, many hours of introspection. What else is there to do in a room that was smaller than many American closets?

But it wasn't all malaria and serious thinking. There were many orgasmic moments, many. Plus the novel that seemed to be writing itself whenever I picked up the pen.

Four long months in a small room. Grace was beginning to edge her rivals over the side of the nest. I could see it happening but I didn't have a name for it. In addition, I didn't know if I liked the idea or not. What is a "Bone Daddy" with no bones?

Susan Amegashie-Ashi, bless her Montessori soul, saved my life from becoming a Fair Gardens statistic by introducing me to Tom Appenteng.

Tom's rich Daddy had given him a three bedroom house in Kanda, Accra, and he was open to the idea of a roommate. From a cell to a palace. Technically, Bone Daddy was still basically homeless, but he wasn't sleeping in the street. Thank Tom for that.

Big house, actually three big houses in a large, cobble stoned compound-courtyard with a giant, gorgeous magnolia tree in the center. It was Paradise.

Tom was what they call a "half-caste" in Ghana. (We always argued about which was the "half and which was the "caste.")

His father was King of Salt in Ghana, the equivalent to a Kennedy in revenue terms. And Tom was his son by an Irish maid. All of the father's other wives were African women (and, I assume, the girlfriends, secondary girlfriends, mistresses, etc.), which placed Tom in a unique position.

He was the "half-caste," non-Ashanti speaking uncle of a quartet of truly gorgeous nieces, and the half-brother of a formidable female who lived in a huge house across the compound.

Tom was, of course, an eccentric. He loved a beer in the evening, fufu for lunch, always (he attributed his hunger to the Akan in himself), and dabbled in a cross-coded collection of odd interests; numerology and astrology were only two.

We clicked. He was cool, I was a diplomatic scribbler and at the end of the day, we both liked to have a couple of ABC lagers's at the little outdoor bar across the road and watched the thousand of bats pepper the air as they started their evening's hunt.

In between times, I sat on my little roomside-veranda-porch, at night, nourished by a dim bulb, sipping local gin and scribbling to my heart's content.

In the afternoons, I might be privileged to scribble and watch the nieces do what they had to do.

The gorgeous nieces made me think of Tom Feelings' paintings. Even during the course of the most prosaic work, there always seemed to be art and grace attached to the accomplishment of the task.

I fell in love with all of them, of course, and held my attraction in so strongly that it almost forced them to break the ice. But they didn't, and I didn't, and thusly, we retained and fed on a tension that gave the sexual vibe a new dimension.

I studied them. I studied their language, their gestures, their clothes, the way they ate omo tuo, the way they ate fufu, the way they swept the leaves away from under the tree, the way they watched me, the way they watched each other, the way they stood.

Four beautiful girls (I think the oldest was 17-18) who sparkled like black diamonds. I took note of the fact that Grace came to visit me, even times when she hadn't been invited. But, of course, she was welcome, she had to be.

May, '93, came like a shot between the eyes. My plane ticket was going to expire, I was going to go into a delinquent visa status. I had to leave, I would have to leave my place to go back to No Place.

Grace came to spend the night with me before I left. No one has ever tried to describe what lovemaking, during the rainy season, in Accra, Ghana, can possibly be like.

I have several concrete theories; number one, all of the Ghanaian writers I've read are/have been so sexually colonialized they blot out what they see and feel, in order to achieve Eurocentric/Puritanical approval.

Number two; writers in Ghana, like writers in America ('til recently) tend to be dry ass-academics.

Number three; I just don't feel that they've ever had a 'hood to 'hood-Bone Daddy view of the sexual picture.

It doesn't always rain during the rainy season in Ghana, but there seems to be a pregnant moisture in the air, even when it's not raining. The lovemaking is silent, there may be people in the next room, the next compound, all quite close.

Stuff can go on and on, especially if the man is an African—American who has come home to enjoy himself.

(Several African-American oralists have been highly placed on a number of hit lists.)

Moist night, everything outside the darkened bedroom window huddled under the flossy leaves and ivory-waxy flowers of the Magnolia tree. Sexy frogs croak (the males, they say), begging the females to come.

We are two quiet, aroused naked human beings, enchanted by our senses. A distant drum signals the beginning of a Pleistocene rhythm. Our kiss lasts for hours. We swim in love, we burst silent bombs inside each others heads and bodies. No doubt in my mind that I had finally found the woman I wanted to spend the rest of my life with, exploring.

But first I would have to leave her, to return to America. Minister/Colonel Owusu had declined to grant me resident status. The big bastard. If only I had had enough cedis to "dash" him.

CHAPTER FIVE

File

Back in the United States of America, California, Los Angeles. Homeless again. A real bummer. My only serious consideration was finding a way to get back to Ghana. Meanwhile, I'm homeless. Well, almost anyway.

"You can stay with me, Bone Daddy, you know that."

Foolishly, I moved in. Four weeks later, wisely, I moved out. If John Outterbridge had decided to say "no," I would've taken a blanket and a bottle of water to Griffith Park. I had already staked out a place.

The lessons that I learned while spending four tortuous weeks in my girlfriend's house will stay with me for life. Number one: some men and some women should never attempt to live together.

They are capable of fighting, loving, sky diving, running, pissing or whatever together. But they shouldn't try to live together. I didn't know that until I tried to live with Lady P.

Number two: don't assume that you are going to be at ease with this person you've always been at ease with, under her roof. If you've been at ease before, you'll discover that she has changed.

"Sorry, Bone Daddy, that's not the way I like to have things done up in here."

And there are other situations that will occur. Each man must find his own way.

The 'Bridge's pad. John Outterbridge, Artist, former Director-extraordinaire of the Watts Towers Art Center (1975—1992), who is generally credited with causing an artistic hullabaloo in South Central "EL-A" during his watch. A friend.

"Well, Bone Daddy, I'm preparing works for a retrospective . . . hope I won't disturb you too much."

I should be so lucky to be disturbed every day of my life, the way he disturbed me. He "disturbed" me for five incredible months.

I would go to sleep at 11:00 PM. and wake up at 5:00 AM., anxious to see what John had created. Creative people are Gods. I haven't had any doubts about that for years.

Those were five of the most "disturbingly" satisfying months of my life. Art is the 'Bridge's life, and mine.

So, I've sold another book to Holloway House, time to go back home to Ghana.

September, 1993. Kotoka Airport, home. Grace was there to meet me. How did she know the time and day of my arrival? I hadn't told her.

I was beginning to suspect that the baby knew a lot more about Bone Daddy than I cared for her to know. Now then, after reasoning all that out, where am I going to live?

Well, this other sister who practically commutes to Ghana, had given me the name and address of a lady named Marilyn Amponsah, a member of the Children's Commission or something like that. I was set for the moment, but I still didn't have my own spot.

Marilyn Amponsah lived on the 3rd floor of an apartment building in Roman Ridge. Osu, Kanda, Labadi, Roman Ridge, I was beginning to know Accra.

In Ghanaian terms, Marilyn had a hip place. As a government employee of some standing, she had a rent free place with running water in a decent area (there were embassies all over the place; the Brazilian Embassy was around the corner and the Algerians were down the road) and a vehicle to drive. A cosmetic check of the scene would have given her situation a big thumbs up. But that ain't the way it was.

First off, the seemingly hip house was dysfunctional. Her two children, appropriately named "Mommy" and "Poppa" in Ashanti, were as delinquent as the circumstances would allow. Her huge boyfriend was a mass of contradictions and Marilyn was a rotten sneak and a petty cheat.

I was not living on sacred ground. The apartment within the apartment that I rented from Ms. Amponsah had some definite advantages. My room had a toilet, which gave me the opportunity to evade and avoid a lot of the family madness.

It took me approximately two days to realize I was living in a den of pirates.

The boyfriend wanted to borrow money from me. I said "no." Marilyn borrowed money from me to buy bread. The "maid," Ama, sneaked into my room to make love to her boyfriend.

The children, uncharacteristically ill-behaved for Ghanaians, tried to borrow money from me. The girl, a conniving twelve-year-old, tried to seduce me. And there was all of the other yang-yang stuff that is customarily found in dysfunctional households— Marilyn avoiding people she owed money to, the children having problems with other children and adults in the building, money missing, stuff.

If they had been speaking English, instead of Twi, they would've fit the frame of any "Negrocentric" family on the Near Westside of Chicago.

And then the brother comes from Sierra Leone, a real slickster who wore two toned shoes, his pants up around his chest, pimped a woman who looked like a small hippo, and asked to use my deodorant once too often.

"No, buy yourself some."

Of course his feelings were hurt, but I didn't give a damn. The whole family had gotten on my nerves. Meanwhile, I'm teaching a Capoeira class at Mr. T's Aerobics Studio, teaching my own Capoeira group of students in Osu, teaching a creative writing class at the Accra Girls Secondary School, teaching a creative writing class at the Ghana International School, writing articles for the Horizon newspaper and the Public Agenda newspaper, writing reams of letters to the people I care about everywhere, writing a novel, trying to figure out how to escape the dysfunctional household (I was experienced now, I knew there was a way), showing my lady, Grace, how much I loved her, drinking a lot of beer and learning a lot at Susan Amegashie's afternoon "seminars."

Yeah, I was busy, maybe too busy, but not too busy to begin to code my way off of the third floor. I was beginning to show signs of bite-wounds.

What's the matter with you, Bone Daddy? Are you going to allow a collection of low grade scam artists to eat you alive?

No, of course not.

Well, then, what's the plan? You can either change your personality around and stay on the frontline of this mess, fight it, or run from it.

I opted to run. I couldn't see a bit o' win happenin' in her house, on her turf.

How did I meet the brother? 0 yeahhh, my Osu Capoeira group gave a demo on Labadi Beach, and he came over to speak to me after it was over.

I didn't pay him any more attention than I would've paid any other shave headed, one-eye-hooded, bright smiling, first African-American-Attorney-to-be-qualified-to-practice-law-in-Ghana.

JaJa Bakari was his name and he became my savior.

"Well, I've got this four bedroom house in Nungua. There's a sister from Philly living there now but she'll be gone next week. I'll be leaving next week, also. I have some business I have to take care of in Atlanta.

"But, hey, don't worry about anything, my man, Kalo, will be there. He'll take care of you."

That's a mild idea of the way JaJa moves. It was impossible to determine what he was doing, on a day-to-day basis, but one thing is certain, he was doing it.

It gave me great satisfaction to see my former landlady, her rapacious boyfriend, her greedy children and her predatory brother washing their hands with distress.

"Please, you mustn't go!"

"Why not?!"

"O, we need you."

"That's one of the reasons why I'm going."

If Roman Ridge was a slice of domestic hell, Nungua was a piece of rental heaven. Teshie-Nungua, never will forget it as long as I live.

Four bedroom house in a walled compound, fresh ocean breezes gently sweeping through every day, even on the muggiest days. A San Francisco high ceilinged bedroom to work in, no domestic clap trap to be involved with.

"Bone, come! 'Dynasty' is on the tellie!"

"Why the hell would I want to watch 'Dynasty?'"

"It's from America!"

And brother Kalo to serve. I have to believe that Kalo was from a different atmosphere. Kalo was JaJa's man about the house, which means that he did everything that had to be done.

And he didn't do it reluctantly. Kalo added a new dimension to the word "servant." He was a servant, but he wasn't servile. He took pride in what he did, no matter whether it was washing the dishes or cutting the weeds that sprouted all around the place.

He set a standard that encouraged me to do better. To try to do better. To do my best.

And there was Grace at my side. I had gradually fallen in love with Grace. Stupid, simple me, after all these months of having this beautiful human being in my life, before I reached the conclusion that I would be a fool not to love her. What could possibly prevent me from loving her, other that my own stupidity?

Nungua was coming to an end, it had to. I was going to be my own man in my own house in Ghana. I had to be. I had spent eight months living in a lovely, ocean breezed environment, but it all belonged to someone else.

It reached a point where I was feeling feverish about the idea. Or was it the latest episode of malaria?

Grace and I decided to pull it together in January, 1995, at the seaside beach resort call Kokrobite.

We talked all day about what our life would be like, together. There were so many things to overcome, to reckon with: cultures, age (I was 58, she was 28), attitudes, two bureaucracies. My visa had expired months ago and I knew I would have to deal with the mean spirited bastards at immigration, eventually. But I would deal with them when the time came.

Meanwhile, there was a house to be built, a life to be lived with Grace.

I was ripped off, but not too badly, doing my first home building deal, anywhere. To have done it in Ghana and escaped alive is a testimonial to the generosity of the Orisha and to God. In a place where the average person is literally living from day-to-day, sometimes from hour-to-hour, the human talent for rapacity can be developed in a way that only a Hollywood agent could possibly understand it.

I had contracted a builder to do me a two bedroom house in Labadi at Palm Wine Junction. It was all set, all of the arrangements made, money exchanged, the whole banana.

In Ghana, with the cheap labor and the proper amount of cement, a small house can be erected in a week or less. We set things into motion in October. By the time April 1995 showed its scarred head, we were supposed to be moving into our place at Palm Wine junction.

Nothing happening. The bare frame of the house was in place, with the beginning of a wall on one side and no roof in place.

I had made an emotional decision, "Come April, '95, I'm going to be in my own place or else." Or else what? I hadn't quite figured that out, but I knew I was going to have to be in my own space. I had lived under JaJa's roof long enough. April 1st, 1995 was my own personal deadline.

Now what do I, we do? The house is half done ("we need three more days, at least") and we have no place to call home. What the hell, we'll go spend a couple days in the Grace Jones Hotel. Our house is only a half mile away; we can go to check on it every day. That's the only way to have things done efficiently, in Ghana. You must sit on the site.

The "couple days" lasted four long months, from February 1st to May 1st. A "couple days" in the Grace Jones Hotel was a lifetime experience.

At the end of a long, incredibly rutted road in deepest Labadi, packed with people doing every conceivable human thing anybody could think of, swarming with diseases of all kinds, was the Grace Jones Hotel.

Mr. Nai gave us the best room in his establishment. It had a shower. We didn't unpack (for the first week), there was no need to do that, we were going to be moving into our own spot in a few days.

Mr. Nai's Grace Jones Hotel was where the local lovemaking was done by the half hour for a reasonable price. We didn't know that when we moved in and it really didn't matter because everybody was cool.

Mr. Nai had a bar located at the entrance to his collection of rooms (Grace called them "money pots") and no one got loud and rowdy, and it was in an authentic neighborhood, which was good for my anthropological research.

But, damn it! I was still living under another man's roof. Four boring months, waiting for our little house to be built. It meant being forced to have a patience I didn't think I had.

It did something for me and Grace that probably wouldn't have happened under other circumstances. We became very close friends. Months in a small space is an interesting way to grow to love someone. Or hate them.

With nothing to do for many hours of the blistering day, we sprawled out on the mattress that I had to lay on the floor to preserve my sensitive back and did soul chats. Or said nothing.

I was enchanted, I am enchanted by Grace's femininity, of her way of thinking, of acting, of being. I felt I was being exposed to a completely exotic trick in our little space inside the Grace Jones Hotel. But I was still living under another man's roof and paying him by the day for the honor.

We had to get out of there. And we did, one bright day in May. What sense did it make to pay rent daily and at the same time pay to have a house built?

My tortured reasoning forced me to see an advantage in living in a partially constructed house (that belonged to me), rather than pay rent for a room that would never be mine.

Mr. Nai was severely pissed to see his "money pot" disappear. But it didn't matter, we were free. I think Grace thought that I had blown my cool, for a minute. And, "Oh," she said, "I see what you've done, you've taken us out of the room and put us in our house."

Damn! I was so proud! For the first time in my life I was living in my own bona fide house, my house, paid for and almost completed.

The finishing touches were literally done over our heads. It seemed to make the workmen work more seriously when they saw that we were going to be THERE.

By the first week in June 1995, we had settled into our Little House in the compound. I have to force my mind to return to the scene to even begin to imagine what our neighbors must have gossiped about.

Here is this middle aged obruni-African-American-writer-man moving into an authentic African neighborhood (there are neighborhoods that are the opposite, yes, in Ghana, West Africa) with a young African (Ashanti) woman.

"What the hell" do you make of it? It was a complex matter. First off, it didn't take long for our neighbors to come to the conclusion that we were not rich folks doing a Harlem/slum scam. We had to get our pineapples on credit too, and eat at Mojays when the cedis grew thin. And I did go and sit in the bar to sip my gins and stouts, just like any other African chauvinist.

Aside from all the regulation stuff, there were some distinctions. Grace didn't work and I had no visible means of income—"he's a writah" didn't mean much to people who were rationing their money for the gift of each day.

Obviously, since I wasn't "working" and "my wife" wasn't working, we were "rich," in some weird, special way. No one could figure it out. I couldn't either.

Those were divine moments in that Little House at Palm Wine Junction, carefully nourished by rainy season midnight thunder sessions and my blown up ego as a home owner.

I wrote in the front room at my little school boy desk, enjoying the children's games that ebbed and flowed from the moment they got home from school until they were forced to go to bed, while my woman prepared jollof rice and delicious gumbo type stews in the kitchen.

We sprawled on the platform bed that I had had a carpenter down the road make and talked about the improvements we wanted to make on the house.

(We had a shower and an indoor toilet installed; a first for the compound.)

We played wari in the bedroom with Grace challenging me to beat her at her own game. I think she allowed me to do it a few times, just to keep the spirit of competition alive.

And we held each other in the bedroom, sometimes like children who felt lost in the world, sometimes to give each other courage to endure the fevers of malaria and other exotic ailments that could only be found at Palm Wine junction, in Labadi, Accra, Ghana, West Africa.

I couldn't see myself living at the compound level, or in Labadi forever, but I knew it was going to take years to build a front porch and to add another level to our little house.

We were designing something (in our heads/conversations, that Home Beautiful would/could never imagine) that was going to be African-African-American unique. And then one night the rain came.

May through October is the rainy season in Ghana, but that doesn't mean that it rains every day at 3:15.

Some days it doesn't rain at all, but when it does, it can rain blizzards of water, huge golicious droplets that can blot out the sight of things a couple yards away.

In July, 1995, on the 4th, it started raining very hard. It rained all day, which gave a moist, pregnant, romantic feeling to the time. And it continued to rain hard, way into the night.

I was going through a malaria episode. Feverish rides on cold swings, marathon sweats, no desire to get well, these little gnomes in their steel plated boots, kicking my temples from within. I dropped my hand over the side of the bed to feel the coolness of the floor, anything to help me get through the night.

So cool, so wet? I leaned over the side of the bed to look at the shallow lake on the floor.

Hallucination. I sprawled back for a moment, smiling. No, I was not going to be fooled by a fever.

I dropped my hand back over the side into water that soaked my elbow. We were being flooded. It felt so cool and pleasant. We're being flooded!

Rain suddenly iced my brain, the fever was gone and we were racing around in our little space, trying to figure out what to do. Cinch the foam rubber mattress with a suddenly found cord, it will float on our mattress-platform. Put a few things on top of the refrigerator. Hop on top of my writing table or drown.

"Bone Daddy, are you afraid of dying?"

It took me a couple wavy moments to answer that.

"It's too late to be afraid." And strangely, I wasn't afraid. My fever was gone, calmed down by the tepid water we were standing in, up to our necks.

From our "ringside seats," standing on the table, we stared through the window slats at the rain, the water flushing into the compound from the narrow passageway that was always so cooly shadowed on hot days.

The rolling of the thunder sounded like worlds fracturing and, periodically, the raindrops would become thicker. Our neighbors were out on their porches, beseeching the gods and God to stop punishing us this way.

The water was at the waist level in the compound; the pregnant woman dashed out into the middle of our neighborhood, screaming, maddened by the thunder and the pounding rain. Her husband and another man rescued her, pulled her back.

She would have drowned if she had fallen. The Obagyes were praying in front of a lantern that cast devilish shadows on their faces. Here and there were signs of panic, but it was contained by cooler heads.

Rain, prayers, people screaming, thunder, prayers, as we stood on the table, exchanging comments from time to time.

"Looks like the water is going down, see? You can see the level over there on the wall."

"The rain is becoming more small, yes."

My all time love took hold in that rain. I stared at Grace's small, sculptured profile and loved her. I loved her for the moments we had shared, the days we had trudged through the blistering rutted roads together, the weeks we had spent in the Grace Jones Hotel, sprawled doggo, waiting for the evening to bring us some relief from the sun, the months we had held each other, not really certain of what the future would give us.

The water surged up under our chins. For the first time in my life I didn't feel claustrophobic in a small space. I can't say why exactly, maybe the water we stood in gave me a different sense of dimensions.

Where do we go if the water continued to rise? We were trapped, and we would drown if the water rose higher. It didn't.

Suddenly the rain was reduced to relative sprinkles and the people on the next porch started singing Christian hymns. We were not going to drown tonight, a night that lasted for days.

We were clearing away rubbish, washing the mud from our walls and preparing to face life again when dawn came. Optimists, we knew that life was going to be better after the storm. It would have to be better.

CHAPTER SIX

KLM (In 'Plane View) . . .

KLM, World Business Class, after two weeks of running back and forth to the airport, to take a scheduled 'plane back to the future.

Back and forth to the immigration, the month before that, blindsided by resentful, corrupt, underpaid bureaucrats.

"We can't allow you to pay your overdue visa fee until you pay your overdue visa fee."

"Huh?"

In other words, if you don't "dash" me, you'll never get on that 'plane back to the place I'm dying to get to, America.

Here, please, allow me to "dash" you so that I can dash out of here. I hated Ghana for a couple of days, during the course of this meanspirited exchange with these meanspirited people.

"Why have you remained so long in Ghana here?"

"Because I love the people, I . . . ."

"That is not a good answer . . . ."

I hated the brutality that their dogheaded processes took me through, the attitudes that permanently stamped them, "Africa, Ghana, Third World." But I kept the whole business in perspective;

I was only dealing with a few anal types, they didn't represent the whole society.

KLM, World Business Class, the blonde placing a tray in front of you every ten minutes, or a glass of wine, or cognac. I spaced out on the treatment.

I nodded, dreamed, cried a few times, thinking about my wife-to-be, back there on the ground in Accra. She couldn't come with me, she didn't have a visa/passport, we weren't married. What the hell, we'd have to do it long distance.

Once again, my most immediate concern was a place to live. Once again I was back in the House, with no Home.

*   *   *

As some of us men use to say, "my baby's Momma" (the women said, "my baby's Daddy") offered me a place to stay in their apartment on Wilshire and Normandie, Apartment 911 Los Angeles.

Talk about being saved. I go from being homeless to living on the seventh floor of a "secure" apartment, complete with a swimming pool on the roof. It took me three months after my arrival to stop trembling.

Residual malaria had me trembling for awhile, plus a sense of unrealness about where I was. I would be tempted to call it culture shock, but I didn't think I had been away from America long enough for that to happen.

This was something else, it was a sense of disbelief. How could I have come from there to this?

It was much easier to identify the source of the tear jags. I was missing Grace more than I have missed anyone in my whole life. I knew I was going to have to fight for her, but I didn't know what the choice of weapons would be, or who the enemy/enemies would be, beyond the concentrated bureaucracies of Ghana and the U.S.

I had to stop crying to get a clear focus on my life, and on the life that I was determined to build for us. It took a few months of stabbing shadows in the dark before I found the proper bodies to shoot at.

Meanwhile, for the first time, I was having the rare experience of getting to know a grandson, a daughter and "my baby's Momma."

"Love," the "baby's Momma" and my grandson, Brian. They gave me a family feast for a year, from September '95 to September '96, I wallowed in the family's bosom. I had never really known "Love," I had just simply got her pregnant, the way boys do at 16, and that was that.

I had gotten together with my friend, the Iyalosa Tanina Songobumni, to have a Somoluruko, an adoption "ceremony for the baby we had," many years later, but I couldn't say that I actually knew my daughter, Gabrielle.

And I could never have imagined a grandson like Brian . . . .

Over the years, "Love" had developed into one of those extraordinary women who had figured out all of the simple emotional stuff, and had a leg up on the complex items. We were acquaintances when we made the baby, and became friends thereafter.

I think of her as the best womanfriend I've ever had. That friendship matured during the year I lived in apartment 911. We talked. She talked, I listened, I talked, she listened. I watched the way she spread her "love" around. It was, to coin a cliche, "awesome."

There were days when "Love" seemed to be feeling whole neighborhoods, sympathizinq with dozens and dispensing advice across the country.

She was/is a composite Oprah/Montell/Ann Landers/Dear Abby/ Yo' Gran'momma, when it comes to advising wisely. Her insights are clear, her advice lush and clean. She did a wholistic number with her positive self.

Our daughter Adesina, "she who brings gold," Gay, gave me a female tinted view of myself. I could see the same characteristics in her that used to make people whisper behind their hands.

"What's the matter with him?"

"He read too much, that's the basic problem."

It was something else with her, a strong sense of reserve, a private person. I connected with her when she gave me a hug and said, "I'm glad you're here." And that was that. No long gushy speeches, no false themes played.

I liked that. I do like that about her, no need to do a jolly-jolly number with her. If she likes you, she likes you, if she doesn't, that's the way that is, no apologies either way.

She typed a fat novel for me, that will be sold by the time she reads this, a serious indication that she cares about me. I love her dearly.

Brian, the grandson I never really got to know. My middle daughter's son, Americhe, Erika's son, or the children of my first delinquent sperm-out. But during the course of one year, I got to know Brian pretty well.

How old was he then? Ten years old? And full of piss 'n vinegar. In my mind's eye I attach a basketball to his hands because I can't ever recall seeing him for longer than ten minutes without a basketball in his hands.

I was called "Grandfather" for the first time and that made me feel honored. Just back from Africa, where titles like that carry great weight.

Apartment 911, lucky numbers for sure. I stumbled around, looking for gigs. I wrote, I made serious efforts to hook up with somebody to make some serious money. I wrote. I wrote to keep my balance, I wrote because I had to/have to, the only addiction I feel safe allowing myself to surrender to.

I got nibbles and quibbles but no solid fix on anything. People promised me this and that but no one came through with anything.

I wrote encouraging letters to Grace assuring her that we would be together again soon. I wrote.

There were times, during that dark year, when I can't really understand how I wrote, but I did.

I know that my mental well-being depended on it. If I stopped writing I would collapse; I wouldn't be able to tell Grace that we were going to have our place (again), despite the fact that I was living in a corner of "Love's" apartment. I wouldn't be able to fantasize correctly.

I wrote. And I'm still writing, with some of the same goals in mind.

I saw a huge black pit open up in front of me when "Love" told me I would have to move out. The lease was designed for a certain number, and I was one too much. Management had taken notice of my rituals on the rooftop and my jaunty air about the joint.

"Bone Daddy" was homeless again. Fortunately, I knew J . . . . Surely everyone should have at least one friend like J . . . .

J., the Packrat.

"Yeah, you got a place here, if you can find a way to get in."

I cast around for other possibilities. I was willing to do any number of things to prevent myself from moving into J's space, what little there is of it.

The thing that you have to understand about J is this; on the outside he appears to be "normal," but this is pure deception. One has to take a peek around the edge of the scenery to see the real person. His car is a bit more clogged with items in the back seat but that's only a hint.

I was forced by circumstances to go into J's space. Come with me . . . .

The place would be as spacious as any street level loft, perhaps a grocery store without aisles, were it not so congested. The congestion starts at the entrance.

The door opens and we are confronted by a curious mix of stuff crowding the aisle. There is a do-it-yourself wall on the left, bulging from the weight of the stuff on the other side. There is a motorcycle parked on the right side of the narrow aisle, and stuff parked on the motorcycle, and stuff piled on top of that stuff. Some of it is obviously useful; the cans of motor oil, ladders, car repair kits, futons, motorcycle helmets, mattress springs and stuff like that.

But how useful are three or four year old copies of the LA Weekly Newspaper and miscellaneous other bits and pieces of this and that?

Before I moved in with J., years before, visiting him, I became so claustrophobic I had to go back outside.

But now it's a new day and I'm going to live in the incredible clutter.

We feel things clutching and grabbing at us as we carefully thread through the jumbled entrance.

It's almost impossible not to dislodge something, or trip over something as we walk the entrance-obstacle course, which is about ten short yards.

Ten short yards of pure clutter before we reach a fork in the passageway. An opening to the left reveals a large room, maybe twenty feet wide, thirty feet long, filled with every possible piece of stuff imaginable.

A stuffed armadillo, a gumball machine, a full-sized ten panel window, photographic equipment (the brother is a professional photographer), stacks of boxes filled with all kinds of stuff, strips of film dangling here and there.

There is a picture window, the kind you'd find in a Mom 'n Pop store, but this one has blinds and a metallic colored curtain hanging in front. Light comes through but there is no sense of its source.

Standing there, looking at the metallic curtain, surrounded by heaping piles of old newspapers, newspaper racks, bags of ancient Chinese noodles, hat racks, a bookcase stuffed with what seemed to be files of some kind, file cabinets filled with dirty clothes, and God only knows what else. I felt like someone stranded on a desert island.

The smaller room to the right is the most jammed of all. A desk that is piled three feet high with paperwork, old photos, books, prints, newspapers, memos on napkins, junk.

In addition to a couple medium sized glass fish-tanks where he keeps his pet lizards. In the middle of all this, he has two living creatures in these glass tanks.

He feeds them what they eat, gives them water and talks to them occasionally. It seems so bizarre.

The next room, also smaller, but with a higher ceiling, might be called the nerve center of the establishment. There is an answering-machine-fax plainly visible under a pile of notes, candy bars, noodle packages, dirty socks, whatever.

The television is centered in front of the weathered futon sofa, with the stereo ground into the same niche. A small computer is mounted adjacent to the television.

Clothes that were laundromated a year ago clutter the sofa, along with piles of junk mail, legal briefs, blankets, foot powder, etc.

J clears a space for me to sit on and we sit there, jammed together like Siamese twins, watching the best of PBS. He loves movies and other visual stuff, as you would imagine a photographer would, and tapes every possible program that he can. It's almost as though he were trying to save TELEVISION.

The racks on two walls are testimonials to his determination to record everything that passes through his hands. He has wonderful Japanese, French, Italian, Australian, African, Hungarian movies and documentaries but it is difficult for him to locate anything because there is no system with his arrangement, everything is everywhere.

Onward to the next room, which is only slightly smaller than the front room. This is the "kitchen," but also a storage space for ancient sports jackets, odd bottles of exotically flavored liquors (watermelon schnapps, peach flavored brandy, chocolate flavored rum, ginger snap flavored whiskey), two year old copies of the L.A. Times, stuff so eclectic that it would have to be seen to be imagined.

The "kitchen" also serves as a shower because there is no bathroom in the place. Bathing is done in a large plastic "boat." It requires a little effort to learn the technique.

I dug a shallow bed from the center of the clutter in the front room and cried myself to sleep every night for a month. I felt so bad about being so broke that I couldn't afford the rent for my own space.

I was so bad off I had to ask J for help. I felt so low.

Funny, complex kind of feeling.

Here I am, "Bone Daddy, the Player," being forced to live in a junk pile, the most complex part of it had to do with J.

He's a real brother, a true friend, a bit self-righteous maybe, but a heart that's this big. The big problem has to do with the fact that whatever he says, that's supposed to be logical, is invalidated by his illness.

Yes, it is an illness and those of us who do not call him on it wind up being part of the sickness. I was part of the sickness for eight months.

I became a part of it because I moved onto the set. I became a participant in the madness when I allowed my selfish needs to overcome the honest urge to talk with my friend, to help him deal with his massive denial of the fact that the environment he has created for himself (for whatever reason) is "abnormal."

Each of us (his so-called friends) chose to suspend judgment of his ridiculous lifestyle (nowhere to sit, three people standing face to face, saving junk mail, plastic forks, spoons, vacuuming a few inches of space in front of the sofa with a mini vacuum cleaner, etc.) because of an affection for him.

This affection for a quirky, giving, generous, complex human being, allows us to get what we want from him. What do I, we want? No critique of whatever our game is. In exchange, we are forced to surrender judgment of who J. is.

Why would an intelligent person stack mounds of stuff around himself? What series of events brought him to this point?

The contradictions inherent to this lifestyle are incredible. He spends lots of time discussing other people's faults, but doesn't see the irony of the dysfunctional living space. Everything in the place is lost.

I was under the impression, for a while, that he knew where everything was. I was amazed to discover that I remembered where some things were. It was so easy to put something down and have it dissolve into the crazy collage we were living in. How often did we search for his car keys, the television remote control, other odd items? No, he didn't know where anything was.

And I could see the manifestations of that lostness in his daily life. The need to be everywhere at the same time, the mania of working to earn enough credit to buy enough stuff to be in debt for, and then to start the whole business all over again.

I felt like a shyster lawyer, discussing the thin threads of a strange case, as we talked about the craziness of the world, standing a few feet from each other because there was nowhere to sit.

I felt almost ashamed of us, sitting cheek to cheek on the sofa, trays placed under our chins like napkins, because there was no table, no place to really relax. It was like having dinner in the center aisle of a crowded New York subway.

The good brother who would get up in the middle of the night to go to bat for you, but could not bear to hear the simplest advice he could hear—"unload, brother! unload!"

Don't you see: by surrounding yourself with things, with stuff, your mind will be stuffed with stuff? It's almost axiomatic. This has nothing to do with good or bad. Or right or wrong. But rather a closing off, a constipating of many of the good vibes that need clear channels to flow through.

I prayed myself out of J's space. They were the most difficult prayers I have ever offered to my Ancestors, to the Orisa, to God. I prayed to be released from the burden of his "hospitality" and my prayers were answered.

I would never be able to string the beaded circumstances together that gave me a spacious, furnished room in WLCAC's

"Spanish House," a guesthouse used by WLCAC for people who are on the scene, doing something for WLCAC.

Well, Cecil Fergerson was the catalyst and Teryl Watkins, the president of WLCAC, was the one who put the blessing on the cake.

"O, you can live in the Spanish House. Rent? 0, well, that's enough . . . ."

So, now, here I am. From a foam mattress on the floor of J's junk pile to a furnished, five bedroom house (all mine when there are no guests around).

From September 1996—April 1997, J's. Now I have space to think, plan, strategize, write. My lease expires in December. If it hasn't happened by then, I'm going to request a full year. During the course of that time I will accomplish all of the things that I want to accomplish. How do I know I can do that?

If I prayed my way out of J's space, I can do anything, even find a cure for my homeless condition.

CHAPTER SEVEN

THE GYPSY IN ME ('Round trip on the Metro to 7th Street Station) Reminiscences . . .

I don't know, maybe it stems from my nomadic childhood, this Gypsy thing, moving from one side of Chicago to the other side (the city only has three sides; the Southside, the Northside and the Westside. Lake Michigan is the eastside). Before I was fifteen we, my mother and sister (Daddy was doing time in Statesville Penitentiary) had lived on all sides of the city, including a stay as far east as the Lake would allow.

I didn't feel put out by this constant shuffling of pads (evictions were the usual motivations for our motions), I was turned on. I hated the ratholes we burrowed into, for a week or a month, but I loved the scenes we wandered through.

On the Southside I got to know a few Japanese kids at Oakenwald Grammar School, over there on Lake Park Avenue (Oakenwald was one of the 18 grammar schools I went to). Where did they come from? I didn't find out 'til many years later, they were refugees from the West Coast, hassled to find some degree of safety from Japanese-haters.

And the pimps and 'hoes (many people say whores). I knew where they came from. They turned tricks and lived in the building we lived in, for awhile, never too long, the Almo Hotel—3800 S. Lake Park Avenue.

In tune with my nomadic side, the neighborhood, the buildings we lived in, the things that happened were never still, never stationary. Yes, the neighborhoods moved. Sometimes they would be Irish or Italian and change overnight to Black. Or Mexican, or Czechoslovakian.

The buildings moved. A four story brick on Monday, a parking lot or a department store on Friday. I was in tune. It was like a Nature thing.

Turning a corner was a voyage into the occult. Going to sleep and waking up in the same bedroom was an adventure.

I crisscrossed the Southside like a White man who was in search of something to "discover." There were moments in time when I was walking through a dream, experiencing the effects of something that I couldn't find a name for.

On the Southside (which included the Lakefront, despite the fact; that it was east), there were collections, aggregations, congregations, glutamates, crowds of emotions, school units, ideas profoundly scholarly and hip men and women. Plus midnight carnivals with so much-much-much-music and life strengthening vibes that it was hard to sleep.

The daytime promised and delivered daytime vibes and the nighttime promised and delivered nighttime vibes, and none of them were sleep invoking. I dreamt of the Southside as though it were surrealistic.

And the same goes for the Westside (where I was born). The Maxwell Street Hospital was where it happened.

Jewtown, they called it back then, and that wasn't considered something derogatory or pejorative. It was where Jews lived, worked and hustled. I think the Jews helped make the Westside my favorite side of town. It may have had something to do with their bread, or maybe it was the Non-Protestant vibe.

It took me a long time to find out where the Jews came from and what a Jew is. If I read the newspapers closely, it seems that they're having the same problems themselves – "What is a Jew?"

I didn't have any doubts about the Gypsies. There was a Gypsy colony in Jewtown, down around Canal Street. I knew who they were, intuitively. The Jews had the bread I liked, but the Gypsies had the soul I loved.

Day after day, I found an excuse to wander through their tiny neighborhood. Maybe three/four hundred people, and I still don't know if they were Spanish, Hungarian, Indian, Russian or what. But that was the drawing card for me, the fact that they never allowed national boundaries to fence them in.

I stared into their mouths when they spoke, laughed at the music of songs I couldn't understand, but seemed funny because the singers made funny faces. And frowned when the sad music was played. I knew the blues when I heard it.

The Gypsies hemmed me in with their stuff. They seemed to be ethereal. They were there and yet they were not there.

Maybe the Maxwell Street Library offered a rationale for my hemming. I'll never know. I do know that it was a Bronzed Age chill racing through the streets, nipping cotton-bound buttocks, that forced me into the two story building.

A library. I was twelve maybe, going on thirty, and had never heard of anything called a library, not on the personal level, at any rate.

A few minutes was all I needed to warm my mittenless hands in the vestibule (a place before you get into a place, my definition of their definition), but that was enough to change my life forever.

Someone was playing the piano upstairs—"Dream Girl, Dream Girl, Awaken to me, 0 beautiful Dream Girl, awaken to me . . . ."

I followed the melody but never found it, or the pianist, and found myself in the Maxwell Street Library.

I have to cool myself out even today, when I recall the excitement of walking into a room that was filled with books. In the warmth of the building I thought I was hallucinating, that maybe I had died in the Siberian cold of the Chicago winter and was reborn in a book-bound Heaven.

Where was the librarian? Maybe he/she was the piano/Circe who lured me into the Room of Books.

I plunged and lunged through the stacks, leaving unread volumes behind me. And wound up with something called, "Romany Rye" and "Lawrence of Arabia."

Only God and the Orisha can say, what took me there, why I picked those books to read, why I heard that melody in my head. "Romany Rye" was a sociological study of European Gypsies.

I can't remember what conclusions the book reached, or what the premise of the book was supposed to be. For me, it was a flight of birds flying higher than any mountain on earth, a glimpse at colors that shimmered in the sunlight.

"Lawrence of Arabia" simply reinforced the romanticism I stumbled into the library with.

I wasn't sophisticated enough to ask the Librarian's help to track down books about the Rom. I just simply stumbled blindly, from one occasional reference to a volume to another.

Everything that I came across served to enhance my admiration for them, for a people who could dismiss borders by roaming the Earth, the way Human Beings should roam the Earth.

During our own "Gypsy period," in two grammar schools out of the eighteen we whipped through, I had two teachers, one African-American and one White who asked me, "What would you like to be when you grow up?"

And when I answered, "A Gypsy," the Earth stopped spinning for a minute. The Black teacher asked my mother to come up for a chat. The chat went on for awhile and I recall the teacher saying something about "identity" several times.

My mother simply nodded, a neutral expression on her pretty little beige face. She knew her son.

The White teacher who asked me the magic question turned slightly pink and stuttered, "But . . . but they don't have any . . . any . . . anything."

"They have Gypsy ways. That's what I like."

The teacher looked at me out of the corners of her eyes for the rest of the time (two months) I spent in her classroom. Guess she wanted to see if the Gypsy in me was going to bust out.

Years later, in Spain, in the city of Alicante, on the southeastern coast, I became friends with a number of Gypsy people and for the first time in my life I realized I could never be a Gypsy. But I still feel like one.

Wandering . . . . Wandering . . . . Wondering . . . . Wandering . . . . Hmmm . . . . reminiscenes.

* * *

CHAPTER EIGHT

Accra

Accra is supposed to be the capital of Ghana, West Africa, but I'm sure that a mistake has been made. Accra might be more than that, it might be a frame of reference for a kaleidoscopic state of urban hallucination.

Accra, Ghana, a kaleidoscopic hallucination. Mmmmm, good place to start. Being a part of it does not make it any less fantastic; realism becomes chained to the surreal, and therein we have the beginning of an understanding (Rastafarian use of the word) about how to describe life in this place.

Buying/selling, re-buying/re-selling. Perhaps three fourths of the people who live in this city are trying to sell something, mercilessly. On some days, everyone seems to be trying to sell something to everybody else.

Arbitrarily; con-men/women attempt to give those who are illusion oriented whatever they feel they need, to feel "complete."

The slicksters are quite overbalanced by the beggars, people who are so completely done in by life that they can't imagine taking themselves to another level. Or maybe they don't need to.

After a few months of walking up and down, I became focused on two beggars. One of them was a woman who looked as though her limbs had developed in spider fashion. She was a daughter of the dust, actually.

The other source of my enchantment was a woman who had leprosy. She frequently claimed donations from me by sneaking up behind me, to present her noseless face for my intimate inspection. I screamed a couple of times and gave her thousands of cedis on each occasion.

Why was I giving her money?

A) Because her nose, fingers and toes had rotted off?

B) Because she made me think of my late, great, Aunt Mary?

C) Because she was so clearly a representative of all that I was being exposed to? I was quite certain, with her visible signs of disease, that she probably was not spending her begged income on well chilled bottles of ABC.

I wasn't so certain about "the spider woman," the daughter of the dust. Passing through her querencia, I was frequently surprised to see her having her hair braided. Why did that annoy me? Why shouldn't a woman who happened to be a beggar-cripple have her hair braided?

I had to let go of a few notions. Just because a woman has a body like a spider doesn't mean that she isn't a woman, or doesn't want to behave like a woman.

The afternoon I strolled past her, my mind on a bunch of other thoughts, was a feverishly recalled day for months to come.

"Hello," she spoke to me. "Hello," I replied, and took careful note of the two young children playing around and about her spidery limbs.

"These are my children," she said as she slithered into a defensive coil. Her children?

How could a severely crippled woman, hobbling along under the power of her knees and knuckles, have children? How could she get pregnant? Who was the man who made love to her?

My mind was fast forwarded and reversed at the same time. Maybe it was the Sun. Or the malaria or something else that I have been infected by, that I couldn't identify.

For days, I was bombarded by those kinds of rhythms. For days I tried to think logically about the things that whirled around me. There were times when I succeeded for a moment, and then I was forced to relinquish that small victory by something overloading it.

I flowed with the flow of Accra, finally, not being intellectual, but careful, observant and feeling.

In the middle of the stench that piles layers of negative thoughts in front of us, there are flower-smiles, magical body gestures that convey a sense of human warmth that cannot be found anywhere else in the world, especially if you are an African-American.

(A word of caution. Many Ghanaians, many Africans are not totally hip to the Diasporans. We may have a certain look, but they discount that and buy into culture.)

If your Twi, Ga or Ewe isn't up to snuff, then you will probably have to suffer with the ridiculous concept of being an "Obruni," an outsider, a European.

Some African-Americans have been so offended by being labeled "Europeans" that they've not made an effort to return to the Motherland.

(There's much more to be said about this peculiar phenomenon, at another time.)

We can put ourselves on Pause, from moment to moment, recognizing Fathers, Mothers, Sisters, Brothers, Uncles, Aunts, Cousins, friends, neighbors, enemies. And they see those same figures in us, but the "Obruni" thing gets in their way and makes it difficult to claim kinship to us, in the way that we claim kinship to them.

Accra brings up all this, all of these things. Strangely, in this place where commerce means everything, sin is not easily found. It is not unknown, but it is not flaunted either, O.K.?

Commerce in many places means selling the human body (sexually); that is not the way it works in Accra.

There is a proper order of things, which may be attributed to the Ashanti domination (pre-British) rather than anything colonial.

During the heat of the day (starting at full daylight) breakfast is sold; waakyi, tea, breads, peanuts, pineapples, fruits. No sex.

(A word of caution: The Ghanaian beers, ABC, Club and Star, have been substituted for what can be called breakfast, with a number of traditional men . . . buying into the idea.)

Those who are addicted to Akpeteshie (a profoundly low grain gin that may be West African Liquid Crack) will have their drink whenever they will have it. They are the vanguard of the dope plague.

But, so far, no one is selling ass for Akpeteshie (1997. Maybe it's changed). Sex is reserved for the night and there is plenty of it. Of course, in a Third World Country (Chairman Mao's designation), with as many smart people as there are in Ghana, someone figured it all out years ago; sex sells better than Kente cloth.

There is no competition, of course, because the Kente cloth market closes down well before the sex market on King Road opens.

Corruption and commerce. Can we separate corruption from commerce? Well, we'll try. But first, in Ghanaian terms, we'll have to define each one, and which is which.

Corruption, in Ghanaian terms, means "dash," a little something that you present to whomever is going to help you get something done. Formerly, as the historian-socio-people tell us, there was a person ("the Otsiame/Linguist") who was responsible for making the citizen's needs/urges/desires known to the uppers and vice versa.

The European takeover knocked the "Linguist" into a cocked hat. Now anyone who feels that he/she can facilitate matters can contribute to the corruption by simply contributing money. And not promising anything.

Formerly, the Okyeame (Otsiame) was a solid figure in the pantheon. He was responsible for doing something, and he did, because his reputation depended on it.

Nowadays, when any underpaid policeman is able to demand a two thousand cedi "tip" at the nearest roadblock, the notion of an "Otsiame"/"Okyeame" levels corruption to the ordinary level. Commerce, driven by corruption, takes us to another level.

Commerce, driven by corruption may be equated to wholesale mendacity, or to be more down to Earth, outright lying.

Accra, on the business level is bursting at the seams with liars. No one is expected to tell the truth, if they can get away with lying. Of course, this is a fact of business in most parts of the world; in Accra, Ghana, it is a finely honed art.

"So, Kwame, we have a deal. You have promised to pay me one million cedis tomorrow."

"Yes, I promise."

Tomorrow comes, for example.

"Well, Kwame, it is now tomorrow. You have the one million?"

"I did not say that I would pay one million cedis. I said that I would promise to pay you if I had the cedis. I'm still chasing the cedis."

And so on and so forth. Now then, in the middle of all this chicanery, there lurk honest people whose word is their bond, whose every action is governed by a strict code of ethics.

The pendulum swings and sways from one to the other, giving the bite of life in the city a rough edge, sometimes a slippery slope always something interesting.

There is a kind of PMS rhythm to all of this, an off rhythm that feels like a soloist soloing with an orchestra of soloists.

And it goes on from sun up 'til sundown. After the sun goes down the rhythms change. There is a night life filled with stories of young girls from small villages who have discovered how much easier it is to make their cedis, selling themselves, rather than selling oranges. Want to hear a story?

They also tell lies.

* * *

From Imperial to Compton Station . . .

The Accra Girls Secondary School writing class will have to remain my plum description of unrequited love.

I still can't identify the demonic impulse that provoked me to go into the school and offer my services.

My inclination could probably be considered perverse, depending on whose point of view is considered. Personally, it seemed to be the most intelligent way to get to know a large number of beautiful young women at one time.

A completely collapsible educational system was the conclusion I reached, after two sessions. Mrs. Gartey, this gorgeous, chocolate skinned woman with the most kissable looking mouth in the world, was my "faculty liaison," but I only saw her for brief, lust filled chats, every now and then.

So, I'm granted total access to fifty gorgeous African females, aged fifteen to eighteen. And most of them are virgins . . . virgins.. virgins physically, mentally, socially, ideologically. Virginal in every sense that you could think of a young woman being a virgin.

No one asked me for a résumé, a copy of my degree, teaching certificate, nothing. I was an African-American who showed up one day and said—"I'd like to teach a creative writing class here."

A completely collapsible educational system. I could have been some kind of Jack the Ripper. I wasn't, I couldn't be. I could only do the class and voyeur.

There we were, in some off room in the system, fifty yards from the girl's dorms on the other side of the graveled road. How many days did I hurry to get to school a half-hour-forty—five-minutes early? Just to fold my arms on the window ledge and casually adore some of the most feminine women I have ever seen.

They strolled, ran, skipped, slouched, paraded in and out of the dorm dressed in wrap-around lapa-towels, white sheets (in emergencies), and a variety of slips.

I never knew that women's underslips were considered decent cover for outdoor wear. There were days when it seemed that the world was filled with pouting nipples, spitting out at my eyes from the top halves of these glittering underslips.

And my students, "my girls" I called them, were coming from these very same dorms. A half dozen times I tried to match up the image of the beautifully undressed girl (that I had just seen from the window) with the green checked skirt and starched white blouse sitting in front of me.

I never made the correct matchup. They seemed to become different people with each change of clothes, but they were all beautiful. Some of them were West African heavy, not fat, but heavy from solid meals with kenkey, banku and dende.

Many of them were thin, almost too thin I thought, dealing with the nutritional deficiencies of their school cafeteria, but they were all beautiful.

They didn't know anything about reefer-rum-wine-beer-sex soaked nights, the kinds of decadence that most high school students in America take for granted. Or dirty pictures.

They were fascinated, and I'm sure they thought I was lying, when I talked about the behavior of the young people in our schools.

"Sah, even the young Blacks behave this way also?"

It took two weeks and four class sessions to answer that question. They forced me, with the plainest of their innocence, to stay away from the glib, the slick, the simplistic.

There was no doubt in anybody's mind, after a full month, that I adored them. And it was clear that they felt the same way about me.

Such sweet love. We did it with our eyes melting, our voices softly seeking the answer, serious respect.

I had designs on three of the eighteen year olds, but a reasonable discussion with myself over a cold ABC gave me the conclusions that I needed.

So, what would happen? I would make love with them, one by one, and it would be joyous. And then what? I was definitely not prepared to play "sugah daddy." And I couldn't really imagine what life would be like trying to explain who Bird, Diz, Coltrane, Miles and Billie had been, amongst other things.

Fatima, Mabel and Esi. They rotated our deeply felt conversations so cleverly I'm inclined to believe that they must have put a schedule together. The conversations took place after class was over and never lasted for less than an hour.

Fatima was the most mature, in terms of vision and physiology. She had eyes like a doe in heat and gave me a lot to think about. "I cawn't stand it, sah, I really cawn' t. Why must you persist in tawlking to me as though I were a child? I am not a child. I can certainly assure you of that. And I do know what goes on between men and women."

I closed my eyes a lot whenever I talked ("tawlked") to Fatima. Number one, I was terribly tempted to stop her from talking by kissing her. Number two, I was utterly fascinated by the rich sound of this Ghanaian-British accent (no pidgin in Ghana for some reason, not like Nigeria) coming from the mouth of an eighteen year old from the Volta region.

My arguments against doing what we both wanted to do were decidedly weak, but supplied just enough barricade for us to prevent ourselves from crawling over.

During the course of one of our final discussions, a few weeks before the end of the term, we fell into each other's arms and cried passionately.

Mabel was more determined than Fatima, but a bit too romantic to be taken seriously.

"Why don't you confess, sah, confess that it's me you love?"

(I could never stop them from calling me "sah," not even when we discussed condoms, diaphragms, pills, birth control. "Yessah.")

"But, Mabel, how can you say I love you? I've never said anything like that."

"You don't have to say it, sah, I can feel it."

Esi made me feel vulnerable because she looked so vulnerable. She was quite short and very stacked and she knew quite well how to use her height, or my height, to her best advantage.

For example, she never failed to have the top two buttons of her blouse open whenever we talked. And she had a breathless way of making these two rich brownskinned orbs of soft flesh palpitate to make her point.

"I know that you care about the other girls much more than you care about me, sah. But that's not important. What is important to me, sah, is that you know I love you and I always will."

No need to lie about it, these protestations of affection from these three young ladies directly, and others indirectly, certainly did a lot to boost my ego. But it was like empty calories. They weren't women and I needed a woman.

Weirdly, I became acutely aware of that need, surrounded by all of these gorgeous girl-women.

They were becoming women but they had not arrived yet, and that kept me honest. I kept my distance.

I often think about "my girls" and I'm sure they must think of me. I'm proud to say that I never had to ask any of them if she still respected me the morning after.

CHAPTER NINE

DREAMTIME IN GHANA

From Florence to Imperial . . . Rosa Park's Station

The smoke was still spiraling up into the sulfite caked clouds of the Los Angeles Basin, the residuals of the Rodney King whipping riots, as we circled out to sea and made a u-turn east for the trip to the Motherland, May 6, 1992.

We lived at Palm Wine Junction in Labadi, around the corner from everything. I used to get up about 8:00 A.M. every morning, two hours after most of the people living in our compound, and walk a half-mile to the Ghana Trade Fair Centre to take a shit.

This was before we had our own personal indoor toilet/shower put in.

I had a double/hidden agenda. I wanted to rid myself of the fufu/kenkey fish and pepper that I had eaten the night before. For some esoteric reason, it seemed extremely important that I clean myself of yesterday's stuff, before I began to sample the magic of the day.

After the crap, in a far corner of the Trade Fair Center's bowels, I did my Capoeira workout. I'm sure I will never feel that sense of wellness again.

Perhaps, as usual, I was a day or two past my latest episode of severe malaria, punctuated by curative Chloroquine tabs and four brutal shots in the ass at the local maternity clinic. Down to the proper body weight and having the agility granted with the weight loss made me feel supergood. Just being alive" after a malaria attack made me feel supergood.

I was in Ghana about a month before I had malaria the first time. It was the malaria, more than anything else, that caused this to be called "Dreamtime." I never knew anything about malaria before I went to live in Ghana.

Malaria had always been a mysterious tropical ailment that caused Englishmen to give up their will to conquer all of West Africa, or a sickness accompanied by sitar music in one of Satyajit Ray's films.

The mosquito that vomited into my bloodstream, that first time, introduced me to one of the world's most horrible experiences.

It's the intimacy of the experience, the personal fever, the personal chills, the pounding headaches, the aching joints, the weakness, the hallucinations. No one could possibly feel this sick but me.

After a few dozen bouts with the monster, I could predict its coming. But I could never prevent it. I took the anti-malaria tabs and all that, but they only seemed to delay the experience.

It seems, for some gruesome reason, some people are going to have malaria, no matter what they do to prevent it. Maybe we are simply the malaria prone people.

After a year of malaria attacks I found myself capable of going into the heart of the matter. I wanted to die, and I did, for fifteen minutes one night.

On another occasion, I climbed into a celestial swing that gently pushed me from the horizon to the sky. I was overwhelmed with the joy of the rush that swept through my being as the soft winds seemed to glisten inside myself.

I was the bell of a beautiful horn, gleaming, brassy, startling the world with incredibly atonal music. Drums polyrhymed my temples as I tried to keep an accent in mind, a One that was going to keep me sane.

When it got too bad, I did some celestial hiking, floating over rocky places as I stared down at grandparents I'd never known. Grotesque images made me scream silently, I think.

Under the influence of the malaria I felt my blood boil, freeze, coagulate. In between the triphammer kicks of the little men wearing steel toed boots trying to kick their way out of my forehead, I felt the total calm that exists in the eye of a hurricane.

Add self pity to the mix and we have the ingredients for a potentially suicidal situation.

I asked myself and I asked others "why not commit suicide when this stuff gets this bad?"

"Some do," someone told me. I wanted to, before the malaria caused me to have temporary amnesia.

"The Third World," that's the designation that Chairman Mao Tze Tung is supposed to have given for that huge cauldron of colored people who are living substandard lives. I would call it Another World.

It is Another World, and therein, everything is topsy turvy. And, without a doubt, it is the people in Another World who make it what it is. The people are fantastic, gorgeous, wonderful, beautiful, intelligent, stupid, all of the things that people are everywhere, except that the coloring of Another world gives them a more vivid cast.

Another World is where everyone seems to accept the unusual as usual. There is no consistent pattern to any of the bureaucratic frames of reference, no way of knowing which way the wind will be blowing, from day to day.

Sometimes the people who would most benefit from cheating won't cheat. But at other times, they may become rapacious. It may have less to do with the economy than with the emotional vibe. I can close my eyes and hear the drums playing in Nungua and Kokrobite. I can smell the rotted rat shit stench from the roadside drain-gutters in Osu, the deadly funk of ol' Jamestown, the red light district of Adabraka, where big butt Ester lives.

A glistening sunlight flickers through the trees, dappling the long walk home in Roman Ridge, creating hot and cool spots inches from each other.

I pause, thirsty, broke, to have a well chilled bottle of ABC on credit in Herman's Tropical Hut Bar.

I walk from Betty's Shalizar Bar in Osu, to Susan Amegashie— Ashi's Montessori School in LaBone, where a well chilled bottle of Star beer is waiting or will be called for.

"Jakob! Zacariah!?"

Kanda, Ghana, and thousands of bats circling the sky above King Road at 5:15 P.M.

And finally, Labadi, where a piece of my soul was chipped away one wet night.

I can close my eyes and hear NaNa's voice, that strange, musical cackling that she spoke in, coated with a heavy chocolate veil of compassion, love and concern.

Dear KoJo Yankah, the brother who gave me the opportunity to write and direct the "Inspector Bediako" T.V. detective series, a first for Ghanaian, and maybe for West African history.

How many times have I been given the opportunity to write and direct a television show in America? Without even showing a glamourous résumé.

Susan Amegashie, before and after she became Ashi, a visionary and the sweetest hearted human being in Accra, unless you mess with her.

Betty Adule Kotey, my savior on so many occasions I lost count. Betty, the woman who pulled me through gates that were locked and chained by malaria; the beautiful person who fed me and talked with so much logic that some of what she said still makes sense.

Brother Kwame, the cynical taxi driver, who gave me hours of rides and shared my prayers.

"The check is in the mail . . . ."

Grace Hlovor, the philosopher-maid, who clearly understood who she was and where her place was, and where my place was.

"Everyone wants to be something they are not or something they think they should be. I only want to be what I am, a maid. I'm satisfied with that."

Oscar Provencal, the Actor. Never could see Oscar being anything other than an actor, with his deeply dramatic voice.

Akosua Abdallah, also an actress, and a gorgeous woman, the essence of femininity, swathed in her diaphanous gowns and robes. As Salaam Alaikum.

Pastor Betty, the Iyalosa Tanina Shongobumnis's double in Ghana. It would be hard to believe that two people could be so much alike and live in two different parts of the world. I never saw Pastor Betty without thinking of the Iyalosa.

They parade across the back of my brain, a stream of warm figures, JaJa, my Osu Capoeira Group, Lina, ahhhh, Lina, the pixie headed White girl who woke me up to the possibilities of White people behaving in a civilized way.

Victor, the Shotokan gentleman who studied Capoeira Regional with me, from Sierra Leone.

Jan, the German from Hamburg, via Rio de Janeiro and who only knows where else?

Doris, the charming bar owner in the Fair Gardens Hotel, who had only two bottles to pour from and made a profit from each one of them.

And always Grace, my love. If I had had any notion that it was going to be such a problem for us to be reunited in America, I would have stayed in Ghana.

The sun, blisters, fungus, okro stew at twilight, small, important pleasures, made larger by the circumstances.

*   *   *

Walking again. Where? Maybe it doesn't matter. Maybe the important thing is to walk and think.

Walking and thinking in Accra requires yogic concentration. Without thinking you may walk too far, or if you are thinking, you might not walk far enough, but it is inevitable to walk, unless someone is driving you or you are driving yourself.

Accra is one of the great walking cities in the world. It is possible to walk from the ocean to Burkino Faso. Or from Jamestown to Kwame Nkrumah Circle without stumbling across one obstacle.

Well, to be absolutely honest, it may not be quite that easy. A number of things may occur; the riptide of human waves may be an impediment, the thousands of people swarming from place to place, without the synchronized choreography of a school of fish or a flock of geese.

There are moments, times when it seems that every individual is going in his/her individual direction. The thing to do is go with the flow, wherever it's going and return to the private journey later.

The sun may be the catalyst for disorientation, forcing the purposeful hiker to pause for bottles of ABC en route to wherever he/she might be going.

Gripping sights might arrest the unwary walker with the intensity of their effects; the leper woman with a hole where her nose used to be. The thousands of cripples, crippled in ways that are seldom seen in the "developed countries." People with limbs that look like spider legs, with movements to match.

Sad baby faces with eyes that have seen so much misery that they can't become any older, they only die and hope to be reborn. Legions of beggars, madmen and madwomen.

Who will ever forget the sight of the young woman who walked east and west on the beach, back and forth, mile after mile, day and night, totally naked, totally insane? What happened to her? Did she drown?

And the insane couple who found each other in Labadi, who ripped live chickens into manageable pieces and ate them?

It doesn't pay to think a lot about what you may see, if there is a time frame involved. An hour's walk in Accra may last a week, a week a month, a month a year, a year a lifetime.

The seasons change slowly, strangely, in Accra. Sometimes it's raining, sometimes it's hot and dry, and then there are in between times filled with the stuff that no season is made of.

Noplease, it may never be possible to get where you're going in Accra, but maybe that's the point of walking. Yesplease

CHAPTER TEN

Malakia, The Braider—Dreamweaver

"I've always been very careful about my braiding, about who I braid, because I became aware, quite early in the game, that there's a bunch of wayward stuff you can fall into, different energy patterns can be laid on you.

"Mmmmm. I love the smell of your hair, you've been using coconut, huh?"

"Every time I wash it, but go on, you were talking about . . . ."

"O yeah, I was going to give you a serious example of negative vibes. I had just come back from doing Stevie's hair for a concert in Dakar, Senegal . . . now you know I put in a good twelve hours braiding his hair, you know how busy he is. "I had just gotten back and I was chillin' for a minute, when I got this call. It wasn't somebody I knew directly, but she was recommended by the friend of a friend, so, I went. Is this music cool with you?"

"I love it, who is it?"

"It's Ravi Shankar and Ali Akbar Khan together. They're both Masters. Shankar is playing the sitar and Akbar Khan is on the sarod.

"Indian music gives me the right state of mind when I first begin to braid, these slow, invocational beginnings they call alaps. Later on I'll switch to some of these Sangare c.d.'s I brought back from Senegal.

"O.K., I'm called, so I go. Beautiful place right over there across the Bay. If it wasn't foggy I could point it out to you. Beautiful brown skinned sister, wonderful light, my kind of music. We got the financial thing squared away and she occupied a modified barber's chair. I took note of that, as well as the appearance of her hair. It looked like she, or somebody, had started braiding and suddenly left off.

"I didn't see any need to get into what that was about, I simply started my preliminary exam to determine what kind of braid style would be best for her.

"Nice set up, she had a tri-cornered mirror deal reflecting the chair so it would be possible to see all sides of her head at the same time. I was really looking forward to getting into it. But then I slowly turned the chair as we were talking and it seemed, for a split second, that I had caught three different aspects of this sister's face."

"Wowww . . . ."

"Yeahhh, it tripped me out for a beat. I didn't want to jump to any conclusions about anything. I just decided to slide away from whatever that was.

"We decided on a Hausa style. I was a little surprised to find out that she seemed to know as much about the style as I did. The literal interpretation of the style is, "You may not see my insides." It's kind of a mystery thing.

"So, I line up a jug of fresh limeade and we begin. I can't remember telling her that I liked limeade, but she had it there for me.

"It took me awhile to really get started because I had to re-braid the half done section in order to have it rhyme with my weave.

"We started up a little conversation, just casual stuff. We were both into soybeans and amaranth. And, like I said, she knew something about the weave I was using.

"I tried to forget that brief glance of three different faces that I had caught in the mirror, but I couldn't. It made me feel a little paranoid. In addition to that, I happened to glance into the mirror about two hours after I started my work and looked right into her face.

"I've tried to find the words to describe that look ever since last year. I just haven't been able to find any word beyond evil. It was a grinning evil look on her face. Satanic. O.K.?

"Now what? I had made a commitment to do this sister's hair, but there were psychic mindsets involved, clearly. I went into my martial arts mode.

"I wanted her to understand that I understood where she was coming from. I can't say that I really and truly understood, but it didn't seem likely that I wanted to go where she wanted me to go.

"Her hair began to wrap around my fingers, it became uncooperative. I didn't think a lot about that for an hour, I had dealt with uncooperative hair before. I could recall a couple times when Stevie's hair went 'downy' on me.

"I called a 'timeout' for us. If we were really going to have the struggle we seemed to be having, I felt I needed a bit of help.

"I turned away from the sister, the mirrors and all of that, and prayed.

"What started off being a straight ahead braiding job was turning into something else. My arms started getting heavy and my fingers were beginning to 'freeze.' Crazy feeling. I wanted to stop braiding but I couldn't.

"The Orisha answered my prayer and helped me disconnect, you know, like detaching a battery cable. You feel any stress here?"

"No, none at all. Then what happened?"

"I excused myself to go to the toilet. I wanted to have a couple minutes to get myself together. She pointed the way down this long narrow hallway. On my way, I opened up the wrong door by mistake and there, in that half dark room, was a sister standing in front of a mirror, with her hands up in front of her like she was braiding somebody's hair. I stood there long enough to really check things out, I was not hallucinating. The incredible thing is that the sister's face look exactly like one of the faces I had seen in the mirror in the other room."

"I would've been freaked out!"

"Well, I'm not gonna lie to you, I was feeling very, very uneasy, but I guess the braider in me wanted to see this thing through, to see what was going to happen.

"I forgot all about the toilet and went back into the other room. The sister was still sitting there with this evil grin on her face.

"She says to me, 'Before we get back into this, let me freshen your drink.' And she got up from the chair very slowly and walked through the hallway. I looked at her from behind and saw something that almost made me scream."

"What?! What was it?!"

"The best description I can give you is that she had a shadow that looked like a huge plastic cutout of a gorilla, you know what I mean? With drooping arms and a giant neck and all. And despite the straight up way she was walking, this . . . this gorilla shadow was scuttling along just like a gorilla.

"I located a telephone very, very quickly and put in a 911 to my man. I didn't have time to explain, I just told him to come and get me! Like now!"

"I heard that!"

"A minute later she came back with a fresh glass of limeade . . ."

"She had put something in your drink."

"That's what I thought. I was not about to have a sip of that, believe me. I put the drink down and got back to her hair. That was really hard to do because I was beginning to feel shaky and scared.

"In addition to everything else, I was beginning to get real sleepy. Strange feeling. About ten minutes later, Kofi was there. You hear me?! Kofi was on the scene."

"That brother is on the job!"

"She seemed to know who it was even before she opened the door. 'Looks like someone has come to rescue you,' she said, with this wicked grin all over her face.

"I didn't say a word, I just gathered up my stuff and walked out.

"'Oh,' I said to her as I started down the stairs, 'it would be impossible for me to braid your hair; I'd never live through it.'"

"'Don't worry,' she replied, 'if I can't get you I'll get someone else.'"

"Poor Kofi was mystified, until I got in the car and told him about it. He made me promise that I wouldn't go to anybody's house to braid again. It's got to be here or nowhere, unless Stevie calls me."

"What time is your wedding tomorrow?"

"At four thirty A.M."

"0, a Sunrise thing, huh?"

"Yeahh, we want to start a new day with each other."

"I like that. I like those kinds of vibes."

*　　*　　*

TO GHANA, WITH LOVE, A SIDE BAR

I've been thinking about you all day. There were several moments during the course of this day when I wanted to stop whatever I was doing and write you.

Finally, the evening is here, and while the rest of the people in my house, on my street, in my community do whatever they're doing, I feel compelled to write you.

I used to smile at words like "heartbreak" and "I love you," that was way back then, during my cynical days, before I met you. Before I met you seems to be a pre-historic time, a time that had no spices in it.

The spices that I speak of come directly from our relationship. The spices are love, poverty, happiness, disillusionment, sadness, joy, the pain of malaria episodes.

I never knew that the rank odor of a gutted road, with filthy drains on either side, could provoke feelings of love. It seems incredible that I could be happy, surrounded by crushed dreams, famished hopes and children who would never have a childhood.

But you made me happy in spite of all the negatives, you made me happy by opening back doors to a collective racial memory that gave my great-great-great-grandparents a frame of reference, a place to come from.

In the rainy season, when I arrived, you drenched me with rain and some understanding of the pain of malaria, I like to think that I was a quick study.

Dearest Ghana, walking miles on village roads that felt like fufu to the bare feet, feeling that I was on ground that wasn't new to me walking, thinking, the sun burning just above my heart.

I became your lover in the squalor of that section called Osu, in the city of Accra. There were no valentines exchanged, no sentimental knick knacks consumed, just a simple embrace, we discovered each other.

I don't have to tell you. I miss you, you know that, I have to tell you what missing you feels like.

It was pure pain for awhile; the jab of a spear in the heart, before the proud flesh created a shield from the weakest of the jabs.

Even with the cushion of reality and proud flesh offering shields there are moments of anguish. The anguish is simple, yet complex.

The sound of hands clapping makes me think of the game that you once played when you were a girl.

Moments when I want to cry from the anguish of not being close enough to hear your voice, to taste your food, to hear the sounds of the Saturday funerals.

Moments that cast shadows of beautiful memories; the water I drank after hours of walking under the sun, the hours I spent at the seashore, remembering thoughts that I was supposed to have forgotten.

There is always a distant drum rhythm in my head when I think about you, a kind of primal love rhythm, a heartbeat. And I think about you constantly.

I say to the people I know, who want to know what to do when they "go back home," I say the most awful things. I feel jealous of them, jealous of the affair that I know they are going to have with you.

They are confused by what I say, puzzled. How can you talk about such great love and in the next breath, put this love down so badly?

I can explain but I don't want to, I don't have to, it's something that we understand and that's the only important thing.

Over here, saturated by whipped cream emotions, public relations, relationships, I yearn to be back in your arms, to know the honesty of real feelings again.

The yearning has gone SO deep that I feel as though another system of veins is circulating tears through my body. I know that I must return to you.

I know I must return to you to keep myself from dying of loneliness, the loneliness born of our separation.

Never knew I could feel like this, never knew what love was 'til I met you. It may take a few more months, but I'm coming back. Mi ba.

CHAPTER ELEVEN

The rhythms of the train, Lina Sappong

It would be hard to imagine that a Lina Sappong could exist in Africa. For the Eurocentrists (that's not really a put down word) she might've been considered a Ghanaian "Holly Golightly," minus the ballet shoes in the 'fridge.

I met her, was force fed, one might say, at the outdoor screening of an incredibly boring European film at the Goethe Institute in Osu, Accra.

I was impressed by the nonchalant way she left her purse in her seat, midway through the pretentious cinematic nonsense we had wandered into, to do whatever she wandered off to do.

Afterwards, for some vague social reason, we were channeled past a couple tables loaded with Guinness Stouts, to discuss the stuff we had just sat through.

Lina reappeared, snatched her purse from the seat (it wouldn't've been there that long in Chicago) and joined me in the Guinness reception line. Her nostrils were flared for some unknown reason.

Sexy woman, that's the first impression. Sexiness oozed from her pores. It had more to do with the look in her eyes (layered by black horn rims), than her shape.

She wasn't what you would call "a fine woman," but she did have a well shaped figure. The long jersey knit dress gave her a smooth look.

"So, what did you think of what you saw?"

She stared at me as though I had said something dirty. Or did the look mean that she wished I had said something dirty? I would become quite familiar with that ambivalent look in the months ahead.

"Oh, it was not too bad." ,

(No one outside of Ghana is ever going to be able to deal with the immense number of tonal qualities that can be lavished on "Oh!")

Now what? We did a clockwise, counterclockwise stroll, our Guinnesses held at port arms, and wound up in front of each other again. A staggered, spacy kind of conversation started in earnest.

She came to see the films at the Goethe Institute every Thursday because they were "windows to the outside world."

It was my first time. And I wasn't impressed.

We fumbled to discover what we had in common. Beyond what seemed to be our ability to chat about ordinary things, it was difficult to determine what we had in common.

Some of it had to do with this opaque quality about her, and some of it had to do with me making an easy effort to preserve my cool.

Within another time frame it would have been quite easy to take matters to a "your place or my place" level, if the vibe had warranted that kind of honesty.

But we weren't there anymore; we were in the bitter grips of a sexual plague . . . alas, 1992, and only the foolish and the crazy were into making daredevil propositions without doing a lot of screening.

Time to go, the Germans were putting us out. "Raus! Raus mit ihnen', raus!"

I strolled to the parking lot with her. Surprise! She had a car. First woman under thirty years of age that I had met in Ghana with a car. Was she rich? Well, maybe not, but the car was certainly an indication that she had a more than average income coming in from someplace.

We agreed to meet again, the following Thursday, unless it rained (it was the rainy season), and if it did, we'd meet the Thursday after.

I strolled through Osu's rutted roads after our handshake and datemaking. We were going to meet again next Thursday, unless it rained. We were going to meet again, for what?

I spent the following week puzzling over that question. We were not planning a platonic relationship, that seemed quite obvious. But if there was going to be a label placed on us, what would it be?

In Ghana, women still hold the reins concerning what the nature of a relationship between a man and a woman is going to be, appearances to the contrary.

At the lowest level, the pussy-for-a-price-lady makes it plain that that is what it's going to be.

The "girlfriend" to the unmarried man. The "girlfriend" to the married man. The "mistress/second wife." The "married woman/ mistress." And on and so forth,

The subtle fringes and flows are carefully tended; it keeps everybody "properly" oriented.

Which means that I had to iron my emotions out and determine what we were going to be to each other. I had to assume that it was on me. The "game" indicates that the man pays for the game, but the women determines how it's going to be played.

Well, she wasn't married, I could assume that because I had met her by herself at a movie. That wasn't a married woman's thing to do.

My status was clear; I was a mature, single, African-American male, back home again, who was not expected to be celibate.

By Thursday I had figured it all out. I was going to ask Lina to be my "girlfriend" and take it from there. I was completely open to whatever after "girlfriend" might lead to, including matrimonial "hiss and bliss," as a cynical matrimonialist once described it. I had figured it all out. I hadn't figured Lina out.

The movie was much better than the last one and we left the outdoor theatre chatting about the ambiguous ending as though we'd been attending films at the Goethe Institute for years.

We were in her car and heading for the beach in front of the Labadi Beach Hotel, complete with a string quartet of Guinness Stouts, before I really had a chance to seriously air my views about what I thought we might come to mean to each other.

We parked in front of the artificial barrier in Labadi, that separates the rich from the poor, the Africans from their beach . . . .

(Malibu is different. The White people in Malibu have an unwritten agreement; if you get enough money, we'll let you in, no matter how dark you are.)

And sipped our Guinness stouts. After the final one, Lina signaled for me to get out of the car, I followed her.

We came to the narrow passageway that was guarded by an incredibly hip ol' dude, who took one look at the full moon glaze in our Stout shot eyes, and asked me, "Hold my gun and I will get you a blanket."

I stood in place, silently howling at the moon, holding "his gun," a large gauged stick, 'til he returned with a woven mat, the kind I have often seen Muslims pray on.

I handed him his "gun," "dashed" him 500 cedis and he graciously allowed us access to Labadi Beach at midnight. We arbitrarily stumbled to the dunes at our left.

It was a primeval evening, humidity as warm as our blood, an African night-sky filled with so much moon that it made me feel as though I was walking under an interrogator's chalky white light.

Who decided where the place was going to be? Was the place decided before we got there?

"Do you have condoms?" she asked in a voice that I didn't recognize. Maybe, I thought, we would discuss what we were going to be with each other. There was no time for that before we "hit the beach."

Minutes later we saw the stabbing beams of search lights (they're called "torches" in British oriented Ghana) rapidly waving towards us. We had plenty of time to realize the gravity of our impetuous, Guinness driven actions; "Oh! You should have used Protectors, this one has spoiled.")

"It is a Protector."

The police/army people, with their beaming lights, arrived anti-climatically. That is to say, after scouring the mat and my pelvic area, they couldn't find any spots of conviction, plus my dominating Afro-American-Obruni speech pattern (Lina was strangely silent) seemed to have an effect on their authoritarianism. They escorted us to the exit and sent us away with a solemn warning.

"Do not come back here to do what you have done again."

I could tell, from the sneaky way the "guard" studied the ground at his bare feet, that he had sicced the police on us. Too bad. I sneered at him, we were too quick for your snitching.

Maybe that was the way they had set it up; the "guard" lets you in for a small "dash" and then notifies the police. If you're caught flagrante, and want to get out of it without a lot of trouble, then you "dash" them.

The "guard," of course, gets a piece of the action for his troubles. In Ghana, unless things have changed incredibly, the "dash" can work miracles. And so, thusly began my evenings with Lina.

She worked in one of the Ministries. I never found out which one, and when she finished her day at the office, she had to have her Guinness.

A mysterious person, filled with unpredictable moods, behavior.

She tells me that it would be quite impossible for us to have dinner (on this particular evening), but, as I slip through the gate to go and have the dinner we were not going to have together, she is parked across the narrow, rutted road, slumped down in the spy mode.

I'm being surprised all the time. One evening, after one Stout too many, she tells me that she has two children.

"And your husband?"

"He is not about."

He is not about. Does that mean he has taken a temporary leave of absence? That they are divorced? What?

Paranoia grabs my attention for a few evenings. What does the husband who is "not about" look like? Why is that man with the reflecting sunglasses, the one with the slashed cheeks, staring at me?

Why is that man following me? Is he following me?

An evening at the Rivera hotel, the sound of the ocean lapping the shore is hypnotic, it's time for us to have a serious conversation. "Lina, I've been doing a lot of thinking about us." A crashing splash creates a watery accent. And immediately afterwards the ocean returns to its velvety ebb and flow.

"Well, tell me what you've been thinking."

"About what?" I'm at sea. What should I do? I want to ask her to marry me. But she already seems to be married. And has two children. What happens to the children when she spends the night out? Does she love me? Do I love her?

Well, what's love got to do with it?

"Lina . . . ?"

The following Thursday at the Goethe Institute film showing.

I was ten minutes late, the film had already started. Lina was seated between two large, dark skinned men. They looked like bookends.

I studied their profiles and body language from across the aisle, discreetly. Were they her husbands? Was one of them her husband? Were they simply two men who just happened to be seated on her right and left? I didn't know what to do.

The wrong move would be terrible. Even if one of the other men was her boyfriend, there would still be a nasty thing happening, for me a stranger, to tap her on the shoulder.

Her boyfriend? I thought I was her boyfriend. But she wasn't looking around anxiously, the sort of thing a person would normally do if they were expecting someone.

What to do?

Indecision paralyzed my intentions, and before the lights came on I low profiled out via the outer aisle. The whole business felt tricky.

I felt confused, low, distressed. What the hell was going on with us? I couldn't put it together. We had suddenly zipped from something (whatever it had been) to zip.

I didn't know where she lived. I didn't have her phone number at the Ministry of whatever. I was miserable about her for a whole week.

It rained on Thursday, film night, a blizzard of water. It took a serious hair of dandelion petal pulling logic—"she loves me, she loves me not, she loves me"—to prevent me from going to the Goethe Institute in the rain.

Another week before the next film. I had firmly packed my program into a neatly paragraphed sentence. "Lina, I love you and I want you to be my wife."

I'll always wish that I hadn't arrived before the film started, before the lights were turned off. In the dark I could have made another low profile exit, but now it was impossible. She gave me that strange-ambivalent look and strolled to her seat behind a bushy faced, tall blonde man. I was devastated.

The ninety minutes of film was a blur in front of my eyes. I kept trying to persuade myself that I wasn't crying. Maybe I wasn't crying, maybe my eyes were simply bleeding.

The film must have been a good one because the gathering moved out slowly, exchanging comments as they made their way to the exit. Lina and the tall blonde man were a few couples in front of me.

He suddenly split off from her. The men's toilet. Now is my chance. I tried to be as casual as my urgency would allow me.

"Lina, what happened?" I tried not to grind my teeth together.

"You didn't come."

"I did come but I thought you were sitting with your husband."

"This one is my husband," she nodded toward the men's room with her chin. I remained in place, like a rock in the middle of a stream, as the other people and her husband flowed onward.

That was the last time I went to the movies at the Goethe Institute.

There were days when it seemed that I had walked from one sector of Accra to another, seamless, dreamy walks.

A mid-afternoon bottle of well chilled ABC at the Shalizar Bar in Osu. It's a warm day, not hot, the sun slowly climbing to a vertical position. I'm walking to Labadi Road, to take a taxi to a friend's house in Nungua.

Sometimes all of the taxis are running on Labadi Road, sometimes none. I catch a tros tros going to Labadi. Why not? I need a haircut and there is this small side-of-the-road barber shop owned by my friend, Mr. Lee Hayes.

(A tros tros is a Volkswagen van that's been converted to a mini-bus. The tros tros stuffs about 20 people into it's interior, plus the driver and the "mate," and is not comfortable at all).

Labadi seems hotter, dustier, a bit more ragged about the edges than Osu, but that's clearly a momentary impression.

I manage to escape the maws of the tros tros without ripping my clothes on a couple of sharp edges but the "mate" manages to hold onto my 200 cedis change. They cheat as often as possible, everybody, ancient riders as well as new blood. O well.

I'm strolling through passageways, over trails, small "alleys" actually (called Lungu Lungu), that only the local people know about. The "alleys" are caked with stagnant wash water, slimy green moss, garbage, people cooking, buying, selling, chickens, children, goats, wash hanging on the lines.

Mr. Hayes sits in the window of his one room barber shop. He greets me, welcomes me.

"Come in! Come in! You are welcome. Long time!"

Once again, I'm standing in the doorway of his shop, unselfconsciously checking him out. He is a marvelous spirit on many levels.

He is sitting on a crate, leaning out of the window to greet friends, tell dirty stories, give instructions, welcome his clientele.

He has a normal body from his head to his waist and from that point his body becomes a spider's body. I've seen this abnormality a lot, like the young woman begging at "37."

He directs you to "remove your shirt and hang it on a hook" (or directs one of his eight children to do the job). He has two "normal" wives. And you are positioned on a low stool between his withered legs as he offers profound commentary on the state of the world and clips your head.

Mr. Hayes would never take prizes as the greatest barber in Ghana, or anywhere else, but he offers something on a spiritual level that no ordinary barber could give. He doesn't complain about life, how poor business is or any of that. He takes care of business and that's that.

I was on my way to Nungua, just up the road a bit, but after the mediocre haircut and the superb chit chat, I'm hungry. I'm in Labadi. Why not go to Mojay's Chop Bar? My friend will understand.

Mr. Hayes tries to return my "dash" halfheartedly, agrees to accept it after I gently insist.

Once again I'm making my way through the Lungu Lungu. We are familiar strangers after a year or so. Some people give me a friendly nod and smile, definitely puzzled by my passage through their secret avenues.

Mojay's Chop Bar is not at all remarkable. In some ways it's like Mr. Hayes' barber shop. There is much more in the place than its reason for being.

Its screen doors open onto a fair sized room with fifteen tables strategically placed. The tables are covered by checkered table-cloths that feel like linoleum.

The floor is slanted downward from the door by a few inches, the walls are covered with Christian posters (St. Patrick, Jesus, Lazarus, Mother Mary, St. Michael, St. somebody else, all painted in pale Venetian Euro-White, and four fans mounted in the ceiling that are as noisy as tornadoes.

(Someone is always requesting that the fans be turned down a notch or two.)

A bar is at the slanted opposite side of the door and off the side, behind a dreary little curtain, "the kitchen."

The menu at Mojay's is simple: fufu and light soup, with fish or goat. Kenkey and fish with pepper. And when you least expect it, okro stew, or palmnut stew.

I will have the fufu and light soup with fish and two eggs. And a cold ABC. Maybe that's Mojay's ace in the hole, the cold ABC.

Some people who have never eaten fufu before they tripped to Africa profess a profound dislike for it. I like it, but I found it odd to "eat" a food that was simply swallowed.

A waitress named Irene caught me "chewing" fufu one lunchtime and sternly admonished me for it.

"What are you doing, sah?! You <u>mustn't chew fufu</u>. <u>You must swallow it</u>. Are you getting me, sah?! You must swallow it."

I sip my beer, swallow my light soup flavored fufu and chew on my fish and eggs. The combination of flavors is interesting and exciting. I am satisfied.

It's late afternoon now. Time to visit Susan in LaBone.

Fortunately, I manage to grab a taxi that's going to Danquah Circle from Labadi Road. I'll come down at Danquah/King Road and walk the six or seven blocks to Susan's on 3rd Norla Lane.

(The scenes I'm about to describe occurred largely before Susan's marriage to Ben Ashi, a dynamite brother in his own right.)

LaBone must be considered "upscale." The homes in that area are quite nice and it literally sits "upscale" from Osu. Susan's in La Bone. Susan is the Head Mistress of the only Montessori School in Accra (imitators lurk just beyond her front gate), and maybe in all of Ghana.

I have only the vaguest idea of what the Montessori Method is, after having been talked to about it for hours and hours. Apparently, it is a "children oriented" method of teaching that gives four year olds the power to read, write and reason.

Her waiting list is two years long, the parents are pleased, the children are happy, but Susan remains unimpressed by her success.

That requires a great deal of self-grounding in a place where titles seem to encourage the title bearers, like everywhere else, to behave like assholes.

She is a short, slender woman with a lovely, humourous face and beautifully beige skin. A self-proclaimed "half-caste" (her father is Ewe Ghanaian/mother is English) who is all Ghanaian.

We begin to arrive after the school day has ended (say, 2:00). We? Who are we? Who were we?

We are the ones who come after the children have finished for the day. And like the children, we come from all parts of the world. Susan welcomes us with Cold Star beer (periodically replenished by her right hand men, Zacariah ("Yessir, madam") and Jacob.

It took me only one week away from the hospitality of her home, her school command post, her "salon," to realize what I was missing.

Yes, the chilled beer on a warm afternoon was quite nice, welcomed with gusto, but it was the freshness and variety of ideas from passionate people, eccentric people, supernormal, intelligent people, that gave those long afternoons such a lovely flavor.

And Susan was the heart and soul of it. Where did she find the energy to spend the whole day running her school (and a number of teachers ragged) and most of the evening participating/moderating/ dealing with all of the rest of us?

I've only had one other time in my life (from 1960-1962) that was filled with as many rich sessions as we had in her space. We talked, argued, discussed, analyzed, rhetoricized, pontificated, learned.

Atheism was the only tabu subject. And there was no argument any of us wanted to give up in favor of having the subject on the agenda.

Above and beyond that, the world was open to explore.

There were evenings when the explorations took such a lucid turn that all of us were made to feel as though we were staring through clear glass.

It wasn't about big words at Susan's, or being oppressively intellectual. It was about pragmatic clarity. The people who came regularly wouldn't permit murky, draggy, intellectual bullying to take place.

Usually a slight, witty nip was enough to coerce the heavyweights back into the people-friendly lane. The nip might become a full fledged bite, if the intransigent deserved that, but it didn't happen often.

John Henrik Clarke, the great African-American history maker/ historian, once defined a civilization as a place where people were civil to each other. There, that was the hook of Susan's place. We were a civilization and I haven't been in an atmosphere like that since I left her place.

*   *   *

CHAPTER TWELVE

While Waiting For The Next Train . . .

A girlfriend, noted for her spacy brand of sarcasm, once said, "Far as I'm concerned, the whole damn thing began to go downhill when they stopped wiping off our windshields at the gas stations."

And Marilyn La Grone Amaral, that magnificent artist-person, coined the term "mean-spirit demon things" to cover the behaviors of the young African-Americans who have diced themselves away from a civilized lifestyle.

I'm using "civilized" in the way that the historian John Henrik Clarke once defined it; "We should not equate industrialization with civilization. We are a civilization when we are civil to each other."

It would have been easy to miss him in a crowd, just another short, brownskinned, middle aged African-American man. He had an interesting face, battered by life, late nights, maybe a few fist fights and one bottle of whiskey too many.

On the Blue Line, trekking north and south, from 7th Street to downtown Long Beach, he wasn't a remarkable character, but after awhile it could have been difficult not to notice him.

Maybe it had something to do with the way he looked at the women who caught his eye. He could have been a champion wine taster with his eyes, the way he seemed to stare at them without actually seeming to do so.

And when he wasn't "tasting" the ladies, he would be staring out at the passing scenes as though he were daydreaming.

And if he wasn't doing anything else, he would be reading. A casual glance at the titles indicated his broad interests. A book on sawtooth wolves, "The Nature of Comedy," "The Middle Passage," "Italians," "Age of the Dinosaurs," "With Matthew Henson to the Pole," "African-Americans," "The Chinese," "The Religion," "Capoeira in Brasil," "Apes, Men, Relatives," all kinds of things.

The people riding the train were studied with the same intensity that he would devote to his reading, anyone could see that.

Now why in the hell would anybody put their shoes in the seat where somebody else is goin' to be sittin'? That's nasty.

Mr. Nelson Garvey Franklin clenched his molars and pressed his lips together as he gazed away from the sight of the young man across the aisle.

Can't say nothin' to 'em, they might shoot you. He smiled at his own fatalistic observation as the train slid into the Slauson Avenue station.

Slauson station, high above the ground. He didn't like the feeling it gave him, to be in a train so high above the ground.

Crazy. I can get on a plane and fly as high as they want to fly that sucker, but here on the train, I damn near get sick to my stomach.

Los Angeles in the summer haze. A young Black man with two big dirty Nikes in the seat where someone is going to sit after he leaves.

Mr. Franklin relaxed his jaw muscles and unpursed his lips. It's like the train being way up here, ain't too much I can do about it.

The thought irked him, why shouldn't I be able to do something? Why shouldn't I be able to tell that young man to take his damned nasty ass feet out of the seat?

He pumped his nerve up to be able to say what he had to say just as the train pulled into the Firestone Station.

The young man literally wiped his feet on the seat and stood up, glaring at all of the people who took notice of his departure, including Mr. Franklin.

And then there was a new collection of malevolent spirits boarding the train.

"Awww nigga! Don't be tellin' me all that motherfuckin' bullshit."

Girls, young Black girls cussin' like that. And the boys talk even worse.

"Fuck you talkin' 'bout, bitch?! What I look like to you, you? A motherfuckin' punk or something?"

One profane word after another struck him as though they were blows with/from an invisible fist. On several occasions, unable to bear the sound of the profanity and all of the circumstances around him—how could they say those things around little children, in front of their elders?—he had simply gotten off the train at the next stop.

"You punk bitch!"

"Fuck you!"

The Black children seemed to be oblivious to all of the people in the train. Mr. Franklin made a surreptitious study of the two teenaged girls who were making the most noise.

Gorgeous young ladies. One African-dark with luscious braids in her hair, the other walnut brown with a pair of silver hoops in her ears. He made an oblique study of their eyes. Dead. Lifeless. Zombies.

It wasn't the first time that he had noticed what he called "the Zombie look." It was most noticeable on the ones who cussed and raised so much hell on the train, the ones who placed their dirty shoes in the seats.

It made an interesting contrast; their animated bodies, gestures, their loud voices, their dead eyes. It was almost as though something had eaten the feelings away from their eyes.

He stared out at the flashing scenery, going behind the wall that most of the people on the train, especially the sensitive, middle aged African-Americans, had to go behind, to listen to how mad their children had become.

They, Mr. Franklin and the men and women in his senior citizen complex in Compton, discussed their young people for hours. Most of them were simply bewildered, a few had theories that made them feel a little higher on the stick.

"Television played a big role in turning 'em into what they've become, ain't no doubt about that." When it reached the point where Black parents were sending their children off to watch television, or allowing them to watch television all the time, things began to go downhill.

"Anybody take a close look at the kinds of poison that's seepin' out of that tube? You'd have to be a superman to avoid being infected by that kind of venom."

Mr. Franklin couldn't find much to disagree with, concerning the "t.v. theory" and in addition, he had diced together a theory of his own to explain the malevolent behavior that they were witnessing.

"I haven't put a precise name on the dis/ease we're talkin' about, but we do know that one of the most widespread symptoms of this dis/ease is boredom.

"Borin' means that something has gotten inside of you and is causin' problems—sometimes people commit suicide because they are bored. Remember now being bored means that something has gotten up inside of you.

"Never heard anyone say 'I'm borin'' unless it's one of those White comedians tryin' to be funny.

"Bore-dom comes from the outside. And it's usually caused by entertainment.

"Or, at a certain level too little entertainment. But I'm gettin' a little bit ahead of myself. Let's back up a bit.

"As we all know, entertainment always comes from the outside and most of it is negative energy.

"A few examples? The television commercials that they fling at our heads night 'n day—eat this! drink this! wear this! get fat! get thin! run! walk! swim! jump! die! – all of this stuff comes at us in a hyper-entertaining way, boosting up the neon light in the back of our minds. And a whole lot of it is aimed at the teenaged market. That's an important thing to remember when we talk about the madness that we're lookin' at.

"Those of us who've been lucky enough, or trained hard enough to relate to info-tainment and edu-tainment in order to be inner-tained, would never buy into simply being 'entertained.'"

"But our young ones, many of them, have never been fortunate enough to have the advantages of inner-tainment; books, serious people talkin', stuff like that."

"Stuff blowin' up everywhere, fifty people being shot in every scene, depraved stuff. And they come right out of that into reality, which is almost a duplication of what they just saw in the movies, the drive by shootin's 'n all that stuff.

"So, now, we got these delicate young minds, already half unbalanced by all of the audio visual junk that's being poured into their systems. Next thing the 'enter-tainers' do is start floodin' their systems with other kinds of 'enter-tainment.'

"The drug 'enter-tainers,' that includes beer as well as the other junk, make everything so appealin' that everybody wants to kick back with 40 ounce of 'kick me in the head' or 'knock my guts out.' With a poison stick danglin' from their lips.

Plus we got these multi-millionaire 'enter-tainers' pushin' their materialism. 'If you wanna jump as high as I can jump, wear these!' Think about it, all of this borin' stuff, all of this outside stuff called 'enter-tainment,' that bores into your mind. When our young people say they're 'bored,' it means that the 'enter-tainment' level has slipped somewhat.

"It means that the heat is not way up there. They're like junkies who were hooked on stuff that was ninety percent pure and find that they can't get as high as they used to be able to get because the stuff has slipped to eighty percent. Or maybe seventy percent.

"Over a period of time, being overstimulated the way they are, they need higher and higher doses of stimulation.

"The prescription medicine to use for this dis/ease is one part info-tainment, one part edu-tainment and two parts inner-tainment, in massive doses, seven days a week.

"Of course, we have to understand, it's too late for some of these 'bored' people.

"Even at fourteen-fifteen years old, they're hooked on 'enter-tainment' and they're apt to be 'bored' to death already.

"Can't cure cancer with a bandaid."

Imperial Station. The short, skinny Black woman, wearing wrap around shades, a tank top over her pert little nipples and a pair of cut off jeans startled Mr. Franklin from his daydreaming. For a minute he thought she was doing some sort of rap.

"Fuckin' goddamn Messicans, Puerto Ricans 'n all the rest o' these wetback motherfuckers, they can kiss my motherfuckin' ass! Who in the fuck asked these motherfuckers to come up here anyway, huh?!"

Once again the middle aged African-Americans on the train made a mental swan dive behind their protective walls.

"Yeahhh! I ain't afraid to say it! Fuckin' Messicans is takin' over. Everywhere you look you see a motherfuckin' Messican! Motherfuckers have three fuckin' babies a year! Goddamn Messicans!"

The Mexican-Americans glanced at the crazy talking little Black woman and then ignored her. A few paragraphs down the Line and a station later, the angry monologue had dribbled to the decibel level of the train's movement.

"So many crazy people runnin' around these days, people with all kinds of problems. This stupid ass race thang. Here we are on the train together, hardly anything but Black and Brown folks on the Blue Line, and this no brain is gonna get on the train disrespecting Mexicans."

He smiled at the memory of another crazy monologue he had been forced to listen to, two weeks ago.

"These young niggers oughta be glad they don't have to have affirmative action anymore, it'll help 'em become more independent, give 'em some idea what White people have had to go through . . . ."

"Shhhhhh! Honey. Please, don't talk so loud, people . . ."

"Don't 'shhhhhh' me, Ella Mae! This is a free country, a White man's got a right to speak his mind."

"But you shouldn't be calling people names!"

"I ain't callin' nobody names, I'm talkin' 'bout niggers. Hell, that's what they call each other!"

The old white haired White man, obviously hard of hearing, continued talking as loudly as he felt necessary from the Artesia Station to the Transit Mall at 1st street in Long Beach.

Mr. Franklin stared out of the window, still puzzled about the feelings he had.

If Black teenagers say "nigger," "motherfucker," "bitch," why should other people be denied the right to say it?

"Nigger." He closed his eyes, trying to blot out the memory of the first time a White man had called him a "nigger."

Chicago, Illinois. 1960. "We don't want niggers in our neighborhood! Take your fuckin' ass back to the Southside."

"Who you talkin' to?!"

"I'm talkin' to you, nigger!"

Hostile people. Defiant people, who are they defying?

Gangbangers. Ignorant people. How could young African-Americans, and some not so young, go around calling each other "nigger" at the top of their voices? Slobs, idiots.

The relentless bombardment of negative images and energies made him feel tired. Damn, no wonder old folks look like they're carryin' the world around on their shoulders.

The air conditioning in the Long Beach Library felt like someone's cool breath on his body. He turned the corner into the first stack, browsing, enjoying the names and titles of the books.

He often thought of the library as a sanctuary in the middle of an ocean of madness. It wasn't entirely possible to escape all of the madness, crazies often occupied tables here and there, surreptitiously sleeping, taking sponge baths in the toilet and shuffling books out of order in the stacks, but they were quiet.

That was the saving grace of the library, they had to be quiet.

He pulled three large picture books from the art section; Picasso, Matisse, Toulouse-Lautrec, three of his favorites, and settled into a reading mode.

Well, one thing that's nice about being retired, and only having a little ol' part time gig twice a week, you have lots of time to go to the library and read.

He thought, and was seriously thinking about finishing the book he had started writing a couple years ago—"Nelson Garvey Franklin's Memoirs—but he hadn't settled into a strict writing mode yet.

Picasso, horny ol' man. Matisse and his dreamy looking women and Toulouse-Lautrec and his whores. The library.

Why couldn't the people outside, the people on the Blue Line behave like the people in the library?

He took his reading glasses off and did a slow pan of the library space. No, these are a different kinds of people, they've come here to learn something, to find out things, to expand their minds, the folks outside don't care about stuff like that.

Three hours of staring at Cubistic figures, Odalisques and dancing girls at the Moulin Rouge seemed like only a few minutes. Mr. Franklin felt a taut rumbling in his stomach, time to get a bite to eat.

He returned the books to their proper spaces and strolled back out into the heat. Just a bit cooler now, or is that my air conditioning armor still on?

Food. Well, I can go home and have something with Marcine or I can get something out here.

He decided to "eat out," to enjoy the flavors of the people.

The Wawa Café on 3rd and Long Beach Boulevard was one of his favorite spots. He had walked into the cafeteria after one afternoon simply because the door happened to be open and the atmosphere was quiet and cool.

He was surprised to discover that the steam table Chinese food in the center of the barn-like room was not too bad, and the place was a harbor for an eclectic collection of men and women, mostly middle aged folks, like himself.

He pulled a tray off the pile, pointed at rice, red cubes of something, a bit of broccoli and ordered a beer from the bar.

Sitting in a window booth he ate his food, sipped his beer and stared out at the people striding past, shuffling by, stumbling, creeping.

Funny how much you can tell about a person from the way they walk. He glanced at the men inside the café. Shufflers, most of them. But they're not hostile shufflers.

He finished his ersatz Chinese lunch and picked up another beer from the bar.

Well, guess I've missed Marcine's overcooked suff today. Lord, what am I goin' to do with that woman?

Ms. Marcine B. Daniels, "the B is for better, like better than . . ."

For two years now, since he had secured an apartment in the Baptist Gardens Apartments ("you don't have to be a Baptist to live here, but it helps"), Ms. Marcine B. Daniels had been his "Ladyfriend."

As the "new boy" in the complex, with most of his own teeth and a flat stomach, he was considered a fair catch by the single women in the Baptist Gardens.

He had simply allowed himself to drift into a relationship with Ms. Daniels, based on a shared need for physical satisfaction.

Wonder where people got the idea that senior citizens don't like to do the do? Maybe they don't know anything about Ms. Daniels.

Mr. Franklin went for another beer. Marcine B. Daniels was a beautiful lover, experienced, gracious, generous, daring. The problem was her cooking, she couldn't do it very well and she insisted on doing it often.

How do you tell a middle aged African-American sister, a Black woman, that she has overcooked the greens? Or that it isn't necessary to always fry the chicken and the fish?

He had made a series of diplomatic attempts to introduce the lady to steaming, baking and boiling, but she wouldn't buy into it. Nor would she stray from pork.

"My Momma put ham hocks in her greens. Her Momma put ham hocks in her greens. And I'm gon' put ham hocks in my greens. This is soul cookin', not Japanese cookin'. There's a difference."

The Japanese dig came from the intelligence source that had leaked the information that his former wife had been Japanese. How in the hell did they find out about Jan? He sipped his beer, slightly buzzed now.

Thirty two years we were married, thirty two gorgeous years.

"Hiya doin', ol' timer?

Mr. Franklin smiled and saluted the ancient mariner who stumbled past on his wooden stump and automatically slipped a dollar into his outstretched hand.

Crip called everybody "ol' timer." How could he call anybody "ol'" looking as old as he looked?

Thirty two years of Janice Sueno Higa. God, what a beautiful life we had. Arguments, yes. Disagreements, yes. Different points of view, yes, but love always.

Why did she have to die first? She was ten years younger. Why couldn't it have been me? He wanted to deny it, but after three years he still felt guilt pangs about her dying. Why did she die first, why wasn't it me?

"Well, as we all know, the Orisha work in mysterious ways." That was another area of conflict between them, their belief in different spiritual systems.

"Now, wait just a minute. No, sir, don't tell me you don't believe in God?"

"I do believe in god, Marcine, I believe in God and I believe in the Orisha."

"Ain't but one God."

"That's right."

"Well, what's these Orishas?"

"Well, they're gods too."

"Uhhh ooh, we missin' a beat here."

Mr. Franklin had to force a loud laugh away from his smile. Marcine was so, so, so earthy. Whatever she was passionate about, she was passionate. And that included her belief in Jesus.

"Are you tryin' to tell me that Jesus is a Orisha?"

"No, I'm not, not exactly."

And on and on and on.

Sometimes he felt that it was hopeless, trying to make Marcine understand how he felt about the Pan-African spiritual system he had been exposed to (Adupe Iyalosha Tanina Shongobumni), what some people called "The Religion."

At the end of the day, as they used to say, when he was stationed in Seoul, Korea it didn't really matter a helluva lot. She was who she was, and he was who he was, and they merged their differences often enough to be considered "a couple."

They hadn't quite decided whether or not they were "in love," but as fully initiated adults, they felt responsible for their behavior toward each other. And sensitive.

Library time was over. He hadn't needed to grab any new books, he was still finishing the last five he had checked out. Time to return for the evening, to the Baptist Gardens Apartments, a senior citizens' complex.

*   *   *

Back on the Blue Line.

Were they crazy or was it just the way he was looking at them? Two tall young Black men had splashed themselves all over the forward section of the car. One had his long legs draped over the back of the seat in front of him. The other one stretched out on the seats reserved for seniors and the disabled.

Mr. Franklin stared at them for a moment, and then directed his attention to other sights. They're gone, po' babies, ain't nothin' can be done for them.

He recognized that nihilistic strain of behavior that stemmed directly from being influenced by wild (non-tribal) wolf culture.

They had nothing to belong to, only each other to depend on or so they thought and what could pups teach pups? He came close to feeling sorry for them. But what good would that do them?

The human waves began to ebb and flow in and out of the car.

The tall young brothers made a loud exit somewhere along the Line, and the train seemed to go into a Zen trance.

Suddenly the relentless reminders of the negative images, the bad vibes, the billboards, the crazy lives they were involved with had departed. The trainload of people relaxed.

Ten minutes later a Black couple entered the train, the woman pushing a stroller with a baby in it. They were in the middle of a made-for-Jerry-Springer-Show argument.

Mr. Franklin looked at their argument as pure comedy, complete with the proper costumes. Why did Black people enjoy having other folks' names on their bodies so much?

"So, you gon' try to tell me you and LoQuita wasn't fuckin', huh?"

"Oooo 'bay bay . . ."

She was a slightly overweight twenty year old who had had a baby for this jive ass boy, also about twenty and he was cheating on her after six months of living together. And she was telling everybody because she didn't have anybody else to talk to.

"I busted you in the act, Leon, how can you sit here 'n tell me y'all wadn't doin' it?"

"Ooooo bay bay . . ."

It was a sad little performance, completely eclipsed by the important events that were happening in the world around them. How could they focus on such narrow issues?

Weren't they aware that the world was in danger of being burned to a crisp on Thursday next?

Weren't they aware that water in Los Angeles had been officially declared "un-drinkable?"

Didn't they know that there were bacteria/diseases creeping through the population that could rot your whole body away in a week?

Had anybody told them about the tobacco cartel's latest moves to addict the Third World?

Did they know that the ozone layer was laid bare, like an open wound?

And that it was literally burning people alive in some places?

Couldn't they see how important humane values had become?

Weren't they concerned about the state of this small globe that had become the world?

No, none of these matters mattered.

"Oooohh, bay bay."

The train bell's clanging announced his station. Mr. Franklin stood and held the metal poles in front of the doors, and as the train slid to a stop and the doors opened, he called out to the Springer couple, "Hey y'all, don't forget to put your dirty shoes in the seats. Remember, other people will have to sit there."

Some of the passengers in the train smiled, intuitively understanding his remarks; most simply looked puzzled.

CHAPTER THIRTEEN

"FAGGOT! PUNK!"

The young man would have been noticed by the most casual observer; a medium tall, body-of-a-ballerina-type, beige colored, and extremely sensitive-photogenic face, Dennis Rodman canary—yellow dyed hair, kohl lined eyes, exquisite dangling gold earrings, beautifully effeminate.

Looking for a seat, anxious to read the latest news before I staggered into the Long Beach Library with the overdue books, I gave much less attention to the trio of young brothers wearing all of the latest labels required to be identified as gangbangers.

One was sitting next to the young boyqueen, the other two occupied the seat in front of them. The thought slipped through my mind—same age, different orientations.

I settled into the mindless mode that seems to be a survival mechanism for riding the Blue Line. Two stations later, the words ripped the air with all of the velocity that an enraged teenager can muster.

"Faggot! Nigggahhh! Faggot!"

The gansta type sitting next to the effeminate guy was bombarding him with insults. We turned to view the action.

Interesting to watch the various postures that the observers went into. Some of us, a bit more sophisticated about negative behavior than others, simply ignored the situation, like we are exposed to behavior of this sort every day, so what?

Others became more interested, but not involved, you could tell from the way they rustled their newspapers and scowled.

"Faggot! Faggots! Faggots!"

The mean teen's language became a litany as he followed/ backed the gay guy through the aisle of the train.

"I'm not bothering you, why do you have to bother me?"

There was something in the young man's tone of voice that made me close the newspaper ("tragedies updated") and give the situation closer attention.

"I oughta kick yo' motherfuckin' punk ass!"

"There are no walls between us."

Once again the young boyqueen's tone of voice conveyed a certain strength, maybe it was the masculinity" of his femininity showing through. Hostility on the Blue Line is often fragmented, like the crazy people who often ride the train, who must chill their madness whenever the train pauses at a station, for fear of the Sheriff's deputies.

"Faggot! Faggot! Niggahh! Git fucked up the ass!"

The strident litany betrayed something about the "singer."

Was he in the closet and felt desperate to assert a masculinity he wasn't positive about? Had he been raped in jail? A common occurrence responsible for the homophobia that infected a number of African-American teenaged boys.

An old white haired White guy with a face that looked like a rumpled bed exchanged eye-thoughts with me. Hmmm . . .

Why was the gangbanger feeling so threatened by the young queen's presence?

"Faggot! Faggot! Nigggahhh! Faggot!"

The mean-spirited boy and the gayboy with spirit stood toe to toe. The mean-spirited one had fire in his eyes, matched by the glare of defensive murder in the queen's opaque, kohl rimmed eyes. The message was silently blazing.

You may take me out but you're gonna pay a price for it, dearie . . . .

I made a sudden arbitrary decision, prompted, no doubt, by thousands of hours of disgust with all kinds of negative behavior, both on and off the train.

I had seen enough, heard enough and had enough. I got off the train at the next stop.

I stared at the figures framed in the train windows, the two young men standing toe to toe in the aisle, the spectrum of expressions on the faces of the people.

The rumpled face of the old White man came into view as the train slid past me. He seem to be saying, "I wish I had gotten off too."

CHAPTER FOURTEEN

Before There Was A Blue Line—
Du Sable High School Football '52-56

I always played football, no matter how cold it was, even if there was ice and snow on the ground. It was like something that was always there, football.

I could play baseball but I didn't really like it, ditto for basketball, plus the fact that I was too short to play center, the position I wanted to play.

Football was my game. And the halfback position was the place I loved. I could run from the halfback position, throw, kick, catch passes and block. Defensive halfback was right up my alley too. Nothing made me feel better than intercepting a pass or making a hard tackle in the open.

On the Southside of Chicago, where it seems that the ball first spiraled into my hands, we played in vacant lots filled with shards of glass, rusty nails, garbage.

We played "touch" on the graveled surfaces of Fuller and Forrestville grammar schools and "tackle" out on the green plains of the big field in Washington Park.

The television screen was mounted in a tiny box then, radios could be listened to on the run, and school was about football at recess.

I had been playing football for ten years before I got to high school.

I had played football with high fevers, stress fractures, a concussion, on an empty stomach, my guts rumbling in the huddle, in the dark against beefy teenagers who had already served their first sentences, and with migraine headaches that caused me to see double and vomit at the halftime.

People talked about me behind my back.

"If he grows a lil' bit, he's gon' be hell!"

"Hell! He's already hell!"

I had a strong arm, was quick as a wink and had heart. I wasn't afraid of anybody. I would try to run around them if I could or run over them if I couldn't.

On defense I would throw himself in the path of the biggest running back, just to slow my progress, if nothing else. I knew very little about the strategy of the game, how to figure things out. I just simply loved running with the ball or knocking down the player who ran with the ball.

It changed for me in 1952, my first year at Du Sable High School, over there on 49th and State. I had picked Du Sable of course, because they were the champions of the Blue Division. They were champions.

I had no real sense of first string, second string, third string. I just wanted to play and set about preparing myself physically and mentally to do that.

During the hour long gym period I ran around the gym. After school, I dog trotted from 49th and State to 38th and Lake Park. And on the weekend, I trekked back to my old neighborhood/Bowen Avenue to play football. I was preparing myself.

"You make the team yet?"

"Season ain't started yet, they won't be havin' spring training 'til May."

Goofing around with another guy in gym one day, swinging on the poles buttressing the basketball frames I fell and fractured my right ankle.

The season was over before it started. There was nothing to do but limp around on crutches and dream about next season. "I went out for the team as soon as they sawed the cast from my leg. Well, I want out mentally anyway. I didn't actually, physically, go out for the team until the Spring of 1953."

Trying to make the Du Sable Panthers, going out to try to make the Panthers was a brutal business. Brutal. The first big problem was the coach. I couldn't tell you what his win-lose record was, for the three years I suffered under him, but I could give you a thick book on what a warped individual he was.

The man was an authentic character, in the sense that such people are always characters. A tall, brown skinned brother with a high butt. He had been a sprinter-hurdler in college and a basketball player.

As a football coach he was an evil influence. Who knows? Maybe all football coaches at a certain level are evil influences. Looking back at him, I see a man who was more a gangleader and a manipulator than anything else.

The evil part stems from watching him encourage us to play dirty football, to be unsportsmanlike.

The people who came under the coach's baton learned how to be excellent players, with good attitudes and well-rounded characters, in spite of the football coach, not because of him.

In 1953, what was I? Sixteen years old, all ghetto hardened muscle and completely crazy to play football. I went out for the team, a loner, not connected to or with anybody. I was almost killed a few times because of the part those factors played in the dynamics of our team.

Several of the players on our team were, well, adults.

A law was passed in 1954 to prevent guys who were 20 years old from participating in high school sports. Prior to that, a number of Du Sable players would "retire" at the end of each football season, and return at the beginning of the next season. It was easy to see why Du sable was the champion of the Blue Division.

And the core of the team was composed of guys who were related by blood, gang affiliation or neighborhood clannishness.

I didn't pay any of it any attention. I just pulled on the old dirty stinking equipment, the sweat grimed sweat shirts, the substandard cleats and dashed out every evening to practice on the gravel.

I tell people that now and they don't want to believe me. I practiced on a gravel grained vacant lot across the street from the school and the practice sessions were as rotten and mean—spirited as the coach would allow, which meant that there was a high tolerance for dirty play.

We didn't wear face masks back in those Neanderthal times and somebody was always trying to stick his fingers in my eyes or bang his fist against my nose.

The playing surface, the gravel itself, was a great ally of thuggish behavior. After being tackled or blocked on the gravel covered ground, it was so easy for the victim to have his face, the most exposed part, pushed or scrubbed on the surface and scarred.

I had scars on my knees, elbows and the left side of my face for years after my Panther days were over.

"The Gang" played offense and defense, and naturally they wanted to stick together, no "outsiders" allowed. I ignored the label and focused on the game. If I carried the ball for a nice pickup and got tackled, I would have to jump up immediately, before one of "The Gang" piled onto me with his cleats showing.

One of "The Gang" stomped on my right toe (with all of his 260 pounds of wine/hamburger/beer fat) and cracked a few bones. I ignored the pain then and for twenty odd years afterwards. Later, when I was forced to have a bunion operation, the doctor stared at the X-ray of my toe and asked, "When was your toe broken?"

The most reasonable answer I could give was that I didn't know. I had to think back real hard because there were so many hurts that felt like breaks. "The Gang" tried to break me all the time.

I didn't take it personally, they just didn't want to see me, or anyone else, break up their little combination. I was a threat.

In scrimmages, someone was always stomping on my hands, throwing punches in the pile ups, trying to twist my ankle, throwing dirt in my eyes.

Strangely, no one simply invited me to have a one on one fist fight. I suspect the reason I was not set up for that was because of what they saw in my eyes. I had made a vow with myself to kill the first person who attacked me, one-on—one.

I was going to kill or be killed, I had decided that.

The coach had the knack of inventing nicknames for everyone, he paid me the great compliment of not giving me a nickname, he simply mispronounced my given name for three years.

The first year was a hazing time, all of what I've described and more. It would have been bad enough if the hazing had remained on the gravel, it didn't, it leaked over into every area of school life.

Du Sable was a jock's school, (it even had a competitive swimming team, unusual for an African-American school, at the time), with a few strong African-American guerrilla-teachers.

Dr. Margaret Burroughs was my personal savior-saint, the leader of the African-American guerrilla-teachers. She was the one who gave me a ream of paper just before the summer vacation and said, "write."

The advice was so unambiguous I felt compelled to follow it. The summer of 1953 I sat at the kitchen table of my uncle's kitchenette apartment house (several people shared the kitchen and toilet) and wrote my first novel.

I had no outline, no plot, no guidelines, nothing but the raw urge to fill up a ream of paper. The novel was about life at the "Peps," that fantastic pre-disco, pre-Hip-Hop dance hall on 47th Street, near St. Lawrence.

The hippest, the coolest, the smoothest made the "Peps" scene. No squares allowed. The primary activity was <u>Dance</u>. We danced the Mambo, the Cha Cha Cha, the Walk, and whatever African-Americans had invented that morning. And midnight.

I'm sure my story was interwoven with tidbits of salacious gossip and lascivious behavior. That's the way I was feeling at the time. But also, there was a lot about football.

I had stolen a football from somebody or somewhere and, in between chapters, I ran around the bridal path in Washington Park (ignoring the patronizing smiles of the horse riders), clutching the football to my side. I had read in a sports magazine that you wouldn't fumble the ball if you practiced carrying it.

Maybe some people thought I was crazy, running around Washington Park, clutching a football to my chest. But maybe not so many; the Southside of Chicago was filled with "crazy" people at that time.

There were dancers who danced all the time, singers who sang whenever and wherever they felt the urge, Poets, Preachers, people who were passionate about what they were passionate about.

Perhaps it was a more caring time. So, maybe no one really felt that I was so much farther out of my mind than a lot of other people.

The football team's influence overlapped, out of proportion. Like, the basketball players were the best in Illinois; Paxton

Lumpkin, "Sweet" Charley Brown, the McMillan brothers, others. The track team had All Staters.

And the swim team was a nugget in the raw, but it was the football team that held everybody's attention.

The football team was the core of Du Sable's sports world. And the "star" members of the team took full advantage of their positions. They robbed, raped, plundered and pillaged. They were high school Huns and most of the student body was afraid of them.

Weird situation. During pep rallies and assemblies, the student body yelled and screamed in support of these bullies who daily terrorized them. And I wanted to be one of them, was one of them, but I had no desire to bully, terrorize, rob, rape or be obnoxious in any of the ways that they were obnoxious.

Well, maybe I should go easy on the rape rap, because that was one of the spin offs of being part of the team. Let's call it date rape, and it was considered ordinary Du Sable football team behavior.

The football players had their grades "doctored," the way smoothed for them to do whatever the coach wanted them to do. It was a really interesting situation that circulated around the coach.

The coach could throw out a number of legitimate basketball players (how can you hide the talents of a 6'9" basketballer?), who never seemed to be able to go very far because the coach had pampered them through so many semesters.

(Oh, did I mention that the coach also coached the basketball team too? He was responsible for messing up a lot of innocents.)

The problem with the football players was more complex. Our "beef" couldn't be graded so finely. It's one thing to have a 6'9" guard who can play forward/center on the basketball court, but quite another number to have a 5'9" guard who weighs 175, who is considered the "best."

He is considered the best in the Blue Division, I always thought there was some irony attached to that because he has been sandwiched between a center and a tackle who are willing to play with as much passion and dirt as he's willing to play, with the coach's encouragement.

Maybe the coach was a sadist. But that would have to be considered a modern consideration. In that place, at that time, he made us laugh at our mistakes, at his mannerisms, at our opponents.

The opponents (a game with Gage Park on Saturday) were least-likely considerations. After a week of vicious, mean-spirited, brutally demanding practices ("break his leg, or he's gonna break your leg!") on the gravel, going into a turfed stadium to play football against guys who were being taught "football is only a game" was really only a game.

The coach was teaching us a lot about what Black life has had to be about which is why I can't outright condemn him, but I still feel he could have taken us to a better place.

I don't know why I disliked the appeal to racial prejudices, as a primeval pep talk. Why was there a need to remind us that we were going to play "the goddamned Jews at Harper," "the fuckin' Pollacks at Fenger," "the fuckin' Japs at Englewood" (they had one playing end) or whoever we were playing that could be ethnically degraded?

I was always shaking my head, asking myself, "What the hell are you doing here?" Playing football, pal, playing football. What else could I say?"

There were days in the harsh autumns of Chicago, when I sat on the stool in the locker room toilet, ignoring the banging on the door, "meditating" on the possibility of being crippled or paralyzed by the activity I was about to participate in.

It was that bad, a psycho football drama that no one could ever know about unless they went to Du Sable.

On "free days," I tripped around to other schools, to sample the vibes (Phillips, Englewood, Hyde Park, Parker). Nothing like Du Sable. In those other places they were practicing to play football, not having war games on a graveled surface.

Scrimmages on the gravel seldom went fifteen minutes before blood was shed, a bone broken, a spirit crushed. But I carried on, fighting off the primitive urge to become like the "others."

Some of the other players began to notice me, to pay attention to what I was doing. On defense I didn't try to rush to be the first to stomp on the offensive player's finger when he was tackled. Or to jump into the unpadded middle of his back.

The coach even took notice. "Are you a Christian or something?"

*   *   *

Hut 2!, Hut 3, Hike!

None of what they said mattered to me, I was on a football high. I was perfectly conditioned. I couldn't overeat because I was poor and we couldn't afford to overindulge in food. And, after my second year, I could actually tune out bad vibes.

It was like having an invisible shield around me. Many times I can recall blocking things off that I was not actually blocking off with my physical body.

Let me give you an example; we were having a tough scrimmage one afternoon, one that was a little tougher than many others, if that's possible.

I was playing right defensive halfback and, on a play called "2-9 power," they were sending all the players on the offensive line to attack the right defensive halfback. The left and right guards came first, then the left and right offensive tackles and finally the center, a huge rascal who charged like an out of control Sumo wrestler.

I played them off to the left and right of my body, like a Catholic priest blessing his flock, and when the ball carrier, a 212 pound fullback named Whitehurst, alias "Pig Iron," came running, I turned him "ass over, buttermilk" as the coach used to say of a great tackle.

My head was always ringing, either from tackling or being tackled. And on the days when I was experiencing this "football high," nothing of any Earthly significance mattered.

Tacklers could butt my body into the air like wild bulls goring a rag doll and I would land like a boneless body, unhurt, untouched. Later that night, walking home, my body would "cake up" and I would feel the effects of the "goring" that I had endured, but it was long after the "football high" was going on. I could ignore the pain of severely sprained ankles, knee bruises, aches, thigh contusions, pelvic crushes, knee shots to the crotch, rib kicks, arm twists to the rear, stompings of the hands and back and one afternoon (shades of the LAPD under Ringmaster Gates) a serious chokehold.

By the time I became a first stringer (in my senior year), I felt immune to pain. In some ways I had become immune to many other things that had nothing to do (directly) with football.

I knew, for example, that it was going to be impossible for the racism of the era (or any other era) to affect me. Which hurts the worst? Being called a "nigger" or being stomped in the back by someone who is called a "nigger?"

In my senior year at Du Sable, I was impeccable. Dr. Margaret Burroughs, a co-founder of the Du Sable Museum of African-American History (she and her husband the late, dynamic Charles Burroughs, kicked it off with exhibits in their home, down there on 36th and Michigan Avenue) had, by this time, become my mentor and my guru.

She made it quite clear that if I was going to be an artist, a writer, I had to be prepared to suffer.

"Being an African-American writer is not easy. It won't be easy. Take a good look at those who've suffered before you."

And I did take a good look at those who had suffered before me. Frankly, I couldn't see a lot to be intimidated by, after all, had I not become a member of the Du Sable High School football team?

Coach Brown has to be given his props. The man was clearly responsible for seeding out the weak from the strong, and was willing to provide the machinery to make that happen.

He was a mean, conniving, egotistical bastard, but he was also responsible for many young Black men surviving.

Some of us used him as a serious problem to overcome. He was there, but we wouldn't allow him to get in our way. And we didn't.

Years after the shoulder pads had been placed on other shoulders, after the boys who had been so mean had turned into tender fathers and dutiful husbands, I stood in the center of the graveled lot where so much of my skin had been scraped off, so much blood shed.

It was a hot, humid, sultry Chicago summertime. A few of the people in the neighborhood strolled past me, not really feeling great curiosity about why this short, stocky guy was staring at the ground as I strolled around the perimeters of the lot.

There were too many people taking weird mental trips for them to feel too much curiosity about another tripper.

In the shimmering hazes of the baking gravel they were all over me, all over the place.

Waylon, the psychopathic behaving brother, who seemed to love inflicting pain. He wondered if the Kharma from that time was responsible for him losing an eye, years after he had terrorized his last sophomore.

Waylon's brother, Richard, the quarterback. Herbert Hagler, "Japan Joe," Luther, Claude "Toy Bulldog" German, "Big Boy"

Johnson, Jackie Sewell, William, Palmer Mitchell, JoJo Carter, Paul Cameron, Karl and Brian Denis, the Twins, Shelly and Ernie McMillan (Shelly played pro ball with the Cincinnati Hawks, or something like that and Ernie played offensive tackle with the St. Louis Cardinals), Lil' Walker.

Lil' Walker, 5'1", was a Napoleon of a linebacker. He was purely extraordinary. He was always in the right place at the right time. And was the surest, clearest tackler on the team.

No one could figure out how he managed to clench the runners by the ankle, like shackles, every time.

The most incredible thing happened. Just before graduation, when colleges began to throw out their bait and/or nets for high school athletes, someone threw out a baited hook for me.

I still get the shakes when I think about it. Miami of Ohio, at Oxford, Ohio, was a small college powerhouse at the time. They had a win/lose record of 150 wins, 6 losses. Or something like that.

The coach was Johnny Pont, who later moved up to Notre Dame. They wanted me to take a weekend trip to Miami of Ohio. I would pay my own expenses etc., etc., but they would take a look at me.

I have only the vaguest notion how the connection was made. I suspect that Coach Finney, a small, barrel chested guy who had played defensive halfback at Iowa State, may have been the one who filled out the form.

I know it wasn't Coach Brown.

"They want you to come to Miami of Ohio for a weekend to see about a scholarship?!"

"That's what the letter said, Coach."

"Well, I'll be damned, son! I figured you to be going over there to the University of Chicago, with the rest of them egg headed Christians."

I'll always have to assume that he offered me his best wishes, after he stumbled past his initial surprise. And it really was a surprise.

A number of the bully boys didn't like it at all, not one bit. Why didn't they get a shot at something?

Well, they would've been able to figure it out quite easily, had they been willing to take a hard, honest look at themselves in the mirror, before or after terrorizing the student body.

Number one, they all had the academic shakes; I doubt if any of the linemen had ever gotten a mark higher than a "C" at any time in history.

Number two, they were physical misfits (with a few exceptions), linemen who were relatively small guys (Waylon, "The Tiger," was a one hundred eighty pound guard) who had managed to play dirtier than everybody else for four years.

(Ernie McMillan played offensive tackle in the pros for years. And a few of the other guys who filled out a bit played semi-pro, but never got to be big bananas).

Oxford, Ohio, here I come. I think the bus trip took about 8-10 hours, my first long distance trip from the ghetto. It felt like a magic carpet ride.

I had boarded the bus in Chicago, surrounded by my mother, father, uncles, aunts, sisters, cousins, friends, warmth and good vibes. Now, after riding through hours of corn fields, the bus deposited me in the middle of a place that looked like a movie set from one of Mickey Rooney's "Hardy Family" series. Or maybe the Ozzie and Harriet family sitcom.

It was Spring and there was something called a "collegiate air" about the place; cobble stone roads, gently waving trees, blonde boys and girls who looked as though they had just washed their faces ten minutes ago.

I stood outside of the bus station, staring at them as they stared at me. I was an "outsider," clearly. They wore polo t-shirts, Bermuda shorts and tennis shoes and I was, well, dressed.

My Uncle John had bought me a suit, a heavy feeling blue suit with a fleur de lys pattern in the weave, three button. I wore a pair of the latest Florsheims, toes pointed like a sharpened pencil, canary yellow, a pair of red ribbed socks and an old school tie that I picked up from a used clothes store.

I had changes in my cardboard suitcase for two whole days, much more of the same. I've take many mental pictures of myself from that day. No wonder the little White kids stared at me.

I didn't feel put down or anything. They were "squares," and who gives a shit about what "squares" think?

Ten minutes later one of the assistant coaches popped out of a station wagon, clenching a beautiful brown pipe between his thin lips, snatched my bag up and began to drive me around the town, and finally around the University campus.

Whatever-his-name-was (I nicknamed him "the Pipe") wasn't friendly, wasn't unfriendly, just businesslike. I asked questions and he gave me answers. By the time I was taken to the dormitory where I'd be spending the weekend, I had the feeling that I'd like Oxford, Ohio.

"Chow is 6:30 P.M. You're on your own 'til 9:00 A.M. tomorrow. I'll pick you up then."

A neat little room, birds singing on the window sill, wowwwww! It would be a kick to go to college at the University of Miami of Ohio. I hung my suit up and tried to dress down a bit in a blood red sports shirt and shine-in-the-dark slacks.

"Chow" was announced by the herdlike stampede of feet shuffling down the stairs and the rumbling in my guts.

I followed the herd to the cafeteria. I was staying in the jock's dorm, I could tell from the sizes of the necks and thighs around me.

Everybody looked like a defensive tackle to me, even the guys who were probably running backs.

The "chow" was pork chop dinners, complete with huge ears of corn, splattered with butter, rice, cabbage, homemade bread, all kinds of side dishes, with apple and cherry pie for dessert.

I sat at a table with five giants, three of them Black. The brother nearest me had six pork chops on his plate, and a collection of other foods. He didn't say a word to me 'til after he had stomped back to the steam table for seconds.

"What're you doing here?" he asked me, between chews. I thought it was an odd question.

"I'm here to get a scholarship."

"O yeah? Ain't too much happening in track."

"I'm here for football not track."

All of the giants at the table stopped chewing for thirty seconds, clearly a sign of astonishment.

Each of them ran their eyes over my body as though they were checking out a cut of meat, a pork chop maybe.

"You too little to play football," the man next to me said in a casual voice, barely disturbing the rhythm of his feeding.

What could I say? That was a thought that had never entered my head. Too little? What's too little? What're you talking about, thick neck? It ain't about size, it's about heart. How many practice sessions have you had on concrete, with gravel top soil? With the "Gang" piling on?

I was so mad I could barely finish the steak sized pork chop on my plate. After "chow" I strolled around the campus, checking out the scene.

It was quite obvious that most of the Black men on campus were either basketball players or football players, and they all had blonde girlfriends.

I saw one Black woman during the course of my two hour stroll around campus; I yelled at her across the acres of manicured grass but she turned to look at me shocked and quickly walked away.

Beautiful evening. I had never been on a college campus before. I really felt like a brother from another planet. A uniquely soft twilight hung in the air for a long time, giving a wonderfully romantic air to all of the activities going on.

Couples were playing after dinner tennis on the well-lit courts. Small groups were strolling the at riding paths, chuckling and giggling about something. Someone was practicing violin. I could see silhouettes in back lit windows, studying.

Somehow I felt a part of it, after awhile. This is the kind of life I could have when I became a member of the football team.

It took me a long time to get to sleep that night, the quietness was so disturbing.

The next morning, promptly at 9:00 A.M., "The Pipe" came for the prospective Miami of Ohio halfback and took me to meet Coach John Pont.

"The Pipe" ushered me into the coach's office, introduced me to the coach and strolled into the sunset.

The coach was a no nonsense type who had dealt with a number of ghetto Blacks who had made their way to his office, hoping to run, throw, block, tackle, catch or fight their way to a better life. Coach Pont wedged himself into a seat directly opposite the would-be halfback and, after a diplomatic few sentences, told me, "You're too small for our program."

We stared into each other's faces for a drawn out minute. The coach had spoken.

I was told that I could complete my weekend stay, if I wanted to, and they would feed me. That feeding was a big thing. But I said no, packed my stuff and had "The Pipe" take me back to the station for the afternoon bus to Chicago.

I couldn't see the point of hanging around after I was told that I was not going to be given a shot at my goal. What would be the point?

The bus trip back seemed to take days, as though I were going through different time zones or something. It *was* my state of mind.

"Too small for our program." Something to seriously think about. If I was not going to be able to play college football after I graduated from high school, what else *was* there for me to do?

Mile after mile, I thought about it. I had never given much thought to life after football.

I took tortured naps and woke up to stare out at a world that suddenly seemed much crueler than usual. I was being forced to make a decision. I would have to retire from football, at the age of 18. No other alternative.

By the time I arrived at our room in the Almo Hotel ("rooms by the hour, day, week or month"), I knew exactly the answer to give my mother when she asked, "Well, what're you gonna do now?"

"I'm going to become a writer."

CHAPTER FIFTEEN

End of the Line

Moments in the Osu Cemetery

A soft wall of silence surrounded him the moment he stepped across that supernatural threshold that divided the Osu Cemetery from the other world,

Across the road thousands of people had moaned, screamed, commiserated with two soccer teams in the National Stadium, the day before. He could look across the curving roadways that led to the elaborately structured government buildings, and imagine how much pain and joy had been suffered in both places.

Familiar names flickered up at him through the dappled splashes of sunlight; Appiah, Kotey, Lartey, Hlovor, Hamabata, Forsdon, Amegashie, Steiner, Reindorf, Brew, Azigi, Nkrumah, Ashi, Brown, Seyiamah, Amartefio, Hayes, Quaye, Annan, Sackey, Wiafe, Wreh, Yankah.

The sleepy men who "guarded" the cemetery saluted him with drowsy waves and silent greetings.

"0, you're here again? Hello. So, how is it?"

He returned their greetings, with equally lazy greetings . . ."So, you're sleeping, huh? Well, why not? Who needs to be awake in a cemetery?"

But he was telling a bold lie. He felt a sense of awareness in the Osu Cemetery that he had never felt in his life. He was forced to conceal this sense of internal ebullience. What would people think if they saw an African-American skipping through the cemetery as though there was something in the place that turned him on?

It was a complex joy. The tranquility was usually triggered by a morning, or mornings that were never tranquil.

He had discovered the Osu Cemetery . . . the tranquility of the Osu Cemetery, by accident.

One midmorning, after a serious Capoeira-exercise workout in the steam-humidity depths of the National Stadium, he stumbled out of the wrong exit and wandered across three lanes of errant traffic, into the Osu Cemetery.

Several of the large, above the ground-rooted trees, beckoned him to their juicy shade. He chose the odd looking one to the left, went to squat on tree fingers that were perfectly molded to his back.

The sweat of the workout, the exhaustion of dealing with everyday life in Ghana, the mysterious headache that was threatening to become a malaria episode all seemed to be sapped from his body by the strength of the tree.

After thirty minutes of "treetment," he slowly stood and stared at the tree, from its accommodating trunk, to the gigantic head that blotted out the Equatorial Sun. He turned from staring at this tree, to the trees that filled the cemetery.

The next day, after his sweat-filled workout. It didn't require much effort to bring up a sweat in Ghana. He stepped across the threshold for the first time. The men who were "guarding" the cemetery looked at him with indulgent surprise. He was obviously an Obruni who had discovered something of interest in the Osu Cemetery. O!!

By now, the names on the slabs of concrete (Appiah, Kotey, Lartey, Hlovor, Hamabata, Forsdon, Amegashie, Steiner, Reindorf, Brew, Azigi, Nkrumah, Ashi, Brown, Seyiamah, Amartefio, Hayes, Quaye, Annan, Sackey, Wiafe, Wreh, Yankah) and the trees that air conditioned the dead seemed to be familiar strangers.

He strolled up and down the aisles, blatantly fabricating life histories and short stories. It was unavoidable.

Grace Appiah, the youngest daughter in a family of seven brothers, must have dealt with a couple of serious, romantic situations in her life. Maybe she had a foreign love affair.

Kotey, a woman of spirit, substance and light, an entrepreneur. Wasn't she the owner of the Shalizar Bar in Osu? Descendants? Wasn't she the victim of inflation and a wounded heart?

Ben Lartey, one of the greatest actors in the world, who said—"To hell with Britain if they don't discover me heah, I certainly won't go there!"

Grace Hlovor, the professional maid; "I am a maid, I know what my job is, I know what is expected of me and I am pleased with myself."

Hamabata, the Fulani broadcaster, on the Ghana Broadcasting Corporation honor roll. The circumcised Muslim woman who sought to raise Ghanaian women's consciousness.

Forson, the akpeteshie drinker. "I had one too many shots of "kill me quick!"

Amegashie. My God in Heaven, did this woman raise the educational consciousness of the people of Ghana or not? Yes, she did. It's in the history books.

Paul Steiner, the Professor. What he did, over there, behind that petrol stations, is incredible. He taught Ga and he taught respect for Ghana.

Rama Brew, an actress. Ahhhh, but much more than that. She took reality to another level because she was a step above real.

Azigi. Well, he could've been the best Capoeirista in Ghana, but he was a serious negligent and loved the flash rather then the substance.

Nkrumah was the best and the hippest taxi driver Ghana has ever produced. The problem is the C.I.A. realized that and had him poisoned. Or shot. Well, whichever, he doesn't drive anymore.

Ben Ashi. They didn't discover him 'til it was tooooo late. Ashi was in possession of spiritual information that he had managed to computerize.

Brown tried to cheat himself aboard an American deal, and failed because he didn't really know what the Deal was.

The student Sekyiamah. She was the brightest and best of her generation. Too bad she died so soon.

Arthur J.M.R. Amartefio, destined for greatness, everyone knew it but Arthur J.M.R. Amartefio.

Mr. Hayes, the crippled barber. He lived the life he preached.

Kofi Annan, who tried to put the world back together and almost succeeded.

Here lies KoJo Yankah, a hero.

He settled himself against the thick trunk of one of his favorite trees and stared, from the mossy shade of the trees in the cemetery, to the blistering scenes beyond the threshold of the cemetery. For a few moments he wondered if he were dead.

The dimensions were surrealistic. Inside the cemetery there was peace, stillness, cool shadows. And fifty yards across the road there was strife, heat, disease, animal passions. Why would anyone want to be out there rather than in here?

His question caused him to smile. Only dead people want to be in here. Well then, what the hell am I doing in here? The complex questions broadened his smile.

He looked around the cemetery, taking in everything; a mother hen and chicks, scratching here and there for food. Two men slowly digging a grave, a hundred yards to his left. A woman with a child walking down the center aisle of the cemetery.

By now, after weeks of pausing to rest, to think, perhaps to meditate, the names and the slabs of marble were familiar strangers to him.

They inspired silent monologues; on this planet we are all searching for a way to know The Unknowable. Competition has given us different names for this search. Buddhists, Catholics, Jews, Hindus, Muslims, Protestants, Searchers, Santeria . . .

He felt no fear of the snake as it made its weaving way five yards away from his feet. A beautiful pattern, green and black, not too large but probably poisonous.

Well, I'm already in the graveyard. He tilted his head back and stared at the branches and leaves of the tree that gave him such a cool place to relax in.

Just the simple things really matter, a cool drink of water, shade from the hot sun, a smile from a friendly person, the innocent laughter of a child.

It was a gorgeous morning, the sky overcast with blue-grey clouds. He sprawled on the marbled top of Kofi's large tombstone and stared up at the sky.

He had pushed himself a bit doing his workout in the stadium by running up and down the stadium steps ten times. Ten times, five hundred steps. He felt his thighs tingling from the exertion.

Man was designed for exercise, for running, jumping, moving around. What does it feel like to be immobilized?

The fine droplets of the rain awakened him from his soft nap. The rain was a soft kiss, a mist being sprayed. He sat on the side of the tomb and looked at the people beyond the threshold of the cemetery, buying, selling, working, playing, living, enjoying the spray.

He closed his eyes and pouted his lips skyward, to receive the misting as a kiss. He had been in Ghana long enough to know that all of the Ghanaian languages had many names for the types of rain that came down during the May-September rainy season.

They would have to call this the kiss-mist. The mist was so warm and sweet that he felt his shirt dampen and dry up on his back. A beautiful rain. He felt the urge to talk to someone about it.

But there was no one there. Well, there was no one that he could talk to.

And the day he had strolled into the cemetery, (forgetting that it was a Saturday, a big funeral day in Ghana), and found himself engulfed by a funeral-memorial-party. He could tell that they had come to commemorate the death of someone, but he had walked into the cemetery too late to see who had been honored.

Clusters of people in funeral clothes (possibly considered unfunereal in other places) circulated through the cemetery. They obviously knew more than one person buried there.

The old man in his rich cloth, with the rich smell of palm wine on his breath, spoke to him.

"My son, do you have relatives buried here?"

The African-American in him responded, "Sir, I have relatives buried all over Africa."

The old man readjusted his cloth and nodded wisely. He wasn't certain that the old man clearly understood what he meant.

The White man-Yellow man-Black man-Brown man-Native American stuff seemed so far away in the cemetery. And driveby shootings, ritual suicides by "space cadets", Wall Street manipulations, the C.I.A., the price of gold, of butter, of all commodities, of all the drummed up dramas that insecure people had designed to make their lives, and the lives of all the people they touched, miserable.

None of it meant anything in the cemetery. The thought made him sit up straight. Why not have the people who were determined to kill each other meet in the cemetery to discuss their differences?

It seemed perfectly logical to him, they would all have to reach the same conclusion; we may not be able to live together, peacefully, but we will definitely be in the same place peacefully, if we kill each other.

The thoughts, the ideas, the notions filtered through the trees, landed on his head, never allowed him to forget that he was being advised by voices he couldn't hear and faces he couldn't see.

No problem. He knew he would be with them in the future. For the moment, he was simply spending moments with them.

EPILOGUE

From the first street station on Pine Street, in downtown Long Beach, across from the library on Pacific Street, to the end of the line at 7th Street in downtown Los Angeles, can be a long trip. Or a short trip, depending on your state of mind. Or how much traveling your mind is willing to do.

The matte-passing-scenery is uniquely Southern California, splashed by graffiti that is also uniquely Southern California, esoteric signs warning one tribal group to stay off of the other tribal group's reservation. Wars are sometimes fought because of failures to pay attention to the graffiti.

The train is a "river," a neutral vehicle shuttling the people who live on its banks back and forth to their jobs, if they happen to have one. In many cases, because racism is still virulent, and they are mostly people of color, they don't have jobs. Or a future, which, unfortunately, some of the younger people are too aware of.

A lot of thinking is done on the Blue Line. A lot of other things happen on the Blue Line too, but mostly thinking happens. Sometimes you can stand in the aisle and literally see thought waves, brain waves, shimmering like heat from a baking pavement.

The people who have people to travel with are animated, they talk to keep from thinking. The rest of us have to face the reality of our minds.

Trains are probably the last refuge for a certain kind of thought process. It doesn't happen in a plane, it's too far away from earth, ditto for the navy, out on the water. But a train is perfect. It's a thought provoker, an avenue to all kinds of streams, sub and otherwise. It's got something to do with the sound of the wheels.

I'm sure that modern sound engineering has had something to do with the seductiveness of the ride. Back and forth, day after day. The people who pilot the Blue Line Trains, (and all the rest of the others), must either be in a rare state of bliss, or completely bored.

The people who ride the train tend to be tame, most of the time. But there are moments when the tension element is elevated suddenly; A Black woman, pissed-off with the world, cusses at the little Guatemalan woman who just bumped into her.

"I wish you fuckn' Mexicans would learn how to walk straight."

Teen-aged hormones create other kinds of tensions, different emotional stuff constantly happens. Seems almost amazing that we can go back and forth, maddened by the stresses of modern life, and not break into packs of killers. Maybe some of the gang members have fallen into that predatory mode.

Maybe some of the people who ride the Blue Line are probably showing us, as a living experiment, that we may not be able to live next door to each other, but we can certainly board the Blue Line and all go in the same direction.

END OF THE LINE